Dragon Fell Farm

By

Lynn Matheson

Table of Contents

Chapter One

1972 Dragon Fell Farm had stood since 1652. The carving above the door lintel announced this fact to the world. It was the highest farm in the Dale, a lonely place where the wind never stopped, and the clouds touched the hill summit. The fir trees in the front garden were bent over like old maids, blasted by the north wind in all seasons. It was as if the house had always been there, carved from the grey stone. It had stood in all weathers, six feet of snow, driving rain and fog that hid everything from sight. Dragon Fell endured. It was built to withstand the climate of the high hills with narrow high windows, long and squat walls and a slate roof. The animal byre was joined on to the main house, not much difference between men and the beasts. All the farms in the Dale looked like this but Dragon Fell was the remotest of them all.

It was the home of the Fairbairn family. The story was that Alexander Fairbairn was given the land as an honour from a local noble. He built it from the local sandstone with his own bare hands. Legend had it that when excavating the land for the house he found a dragon skull. This explained the name of the house. Nobody knew where this skull now resided. Perhaps it was still deep in the foundations or the walls protecting the farm from harm. Dragon Fell had survived. It had withstood wars, storms, births, deaths, weddings and funerals. It had seen great kings and queens come and go in the land. Generations of Fairbairns have lived out their lives here at Dragon Fell in the North Pennines of England. The farm lay in Odinsdale. Some said the dale was in Yorkshire, some in County Durham. The penpushers liked to redraw the boundary from time to time. The dragon did not care. She protected the farm. No infant had ever died in childhood at Dragon Fell. Every Fairbairn male had lived to old age safe behind the solid walls. The women had not been so lucky. Many had died in childbirth. Something was afoot in the land. Evil was stirring in the depths. Odinsdale was changing. The dragon was not sure she could continue to protect the Fairbairns. The dark forces were growing stronger. The old ways were being forgotten. There had been disruption of the Earth in Odinsdale. A dam had been built and there was a new reservoir not far from the farm. The Old Ones had been disturbed. The ley lines were disrupted. The crackle of the electricity pylons lower in the Dale disturbed the peace of the spirits. The Fey liked the moors just as they had always been. They had no love for modernity. Things should be let be.

There was a time when dragons and giants walked the Earth. Though nobody believed it now, it was true. The veil was thin between the worlds in those days. The fallen angels walked the land, and their offspring were giants. The red dragons helped the giants and the people of the Earth. There were women who could charm them and use their magic for good or ill. As men became many, the dragons withdrew from the Earth apart from in the high and lonely places like Odinsdale. They are still there in the other world, and you can ask them for help to this day. The red dragons fight for the Light in the spiritual plane. They toil against unspeakable creatures, the demons of the dark. Every human must make their choice: good or evil. Through choices they grow and learn.

As our story begins the year was 1972 in the year of Our Lord. Draw closer and I will tell you a tale of great love but also revenge and evil things. Both good and bad must exist on the Earth. This is how it always has been and must be. There is light and there is dark.

As our tale unfolds, we see Anna leaving by the front door. Anna was seven years old, and she had grown strong and lively. She walked quickly to the barn to feed her pony Stanley. It was only November, but winter had come early to Odinsdale as it often did. A blizzard had occurred overnight and much of the farm was now covered in five-foot drifts. Her brother, Philip, now a strapping lad of fourteen, was out retrieving the sheep from being buried in the snow with his two sheep dogs, worthy and Hunter. Their father, Alfred, was away working on an oil rig some place far away. He had to take work to make enough money to feed his children. The farm had two hundred head of sheep and twenty cattle, but it was still hard to make ends meet. He was due back any day now.

As Anna walked to the barn the wind bit into her face like a starving animal. Anna paid the wind no mind. It was a constant part of her reality and she had known nothing else. The snow crunched pleasingly under her rubber wellingtons. Anna patted herself to keep warm as she walked. As she entered the barn Stanley snickered a greeting. He was a black Fell pony. Many of his kind still lived wild on the hills. Stanley had been tamed as a foal and was quiet as any lamb now. Anna cut open a bale of hay and placed some of it in Stanley's manger. She separated the strands expertly from long practice. Stanley nuzzled into her in thanks, and she found half an apple in her pocket to give him. Anna moved a strand of her red hair from her face that had escaped from her untidy plaits. She spent a good half an hour grooming Stanley with a dandy brush. She removed the mud with long, firm strokes. Then she combed out his long mane and tail. She chose another softer brush and kept working on his coat until it shone. Anna sang to Stanley all the while. She knew folk songs that her father had taught her: tales of love and loss, war and sorrow. Stanley's ears moved back and forwards as he listened to her song.

She left Stanley and walked to the aviary. Inside was a hawk. He was just called Hawk. Anna had found him on the moor with a broken wing and nursed him back to health. She fed him some dead chicks from a metal bin and watched in fascination as he devoured each one, ripping them apart with teeth and claw. The violence of Hawk both repulsed and enthralled her. In better weather she would have taken him out to hunt but not today. It was too fresh even for the wild bird.

Anna trudged back to the farmhouse, out of the barn door and along the path lined with the straggly gooseberry bushes to the main house. Her fingers were hurting with the cold, and she blew on them fruitlessly. She knew she had left her gloves somewhere around here. She must find them one day before her fingers froze off.

Back inside the house she was straight into the living room or 'the house' as they called it in these parts. The room served as both living quarters and kitchen. Creeping modernity had not reached Dragon Fell Farm. There was no electricity as the electric company had quoted too high a price for connection. The water had to be carried from the spring. There was not even a road leading to Dragon Fell. Vehicles left supplies at the gate two fields down the hill where a single-track road snaked by. The only way down to the road was on foot or horseback along the muddy path. The post was left in a box next to the gate where food supplies were also delivered. They would receive cheap cuts of meat from the butcher, flour, tins of spam and corn beef, pats of lard, potatoes and cabbages from the village shop. Food was simple. In the summer, they grew vegetables and collected fruit from the trees in autumn. Heating was from fires and the old range in the kitchen. There was no bathroom, and the earthen toilet was outside. The kitchen range was black and full of different compartments that stretched up to the ceiling. Anna went straight to it and warmed her hands. She could smell stew from the oven and fresh bread was cooling on the rack. A clatter of brooms falling on to the stone flags announced the entrance of Pearl from the back of the house.

Pearl was a tall, gangly awkward girl of seventeen with a face that looked slightly caved in. She was often referred to as 'not right' by those in the Dale who should have known better. Rumours abounded her mother had drunk half a bottle of whisky a day during pregnancy or that her unknown father had been an escapee from the asylum, but nobody knew for sure. Pearl did the housework at Dragon Fell and anything else anyone set her to. She helped bring the water, washed the clothes in the huge sink and pushed them through the mangle, fed the dogs, scythed hay in the summertime and generally worked herself to a wisp. She lived in during the week and went home at weekends to her mother who lived in a cottage two miles away and spent most of her time in bed with a headache. Pearl walked all the way there and back with no complaint.

"Anna is tha cold lass?" she asked while retrieving the stew and setting it on to the wooden table.

"Of course, I am Pearl. It's a wicked night out there and I wonder when the old man will be back. I expected him before now."

"Aye. I hope nothing's wrong. Philip is still out looking for the sheep. There's plenty of stew to warm you up."

"Thanks Pearl. You are a treasure. I hope Philip is okay. It's dangerous work on such a night as this. I'm looking forward to the old man coming back. He said he would buy me a present. What do you think it will be?"

"What about one of those dolls that can talk? That would be a fine thing."

"Yes, Pearl. I'd love that or a silver necklace with my name on."

Anna set about her stew with gusto. There were pieces of gristly meat with potato and turnip. Steam rose from the bowl. Anna helped herself to hunks of homemade bread and slathered them with butter. The door banged and Philip entered almost frozen and covered with snow. He stamped his feet in front of the range, swearing loudly all the while.

"I'm done. I'm done," he said, removing his boots while sitting at the table.

Pearl set a bowl of the stew in front of him, and Philip wolfed it down without speaking further. He had spent the last few hours pulling sheep out of drifts and driving them to the safety of the fold barn. On finishing, he moved to the high-backed armchair in the other half of the room and closed his eyes. The fire here was roaring in the grate and the dogs laid down in front of it exhausted.

The room was lit with oil lamps and candles that gave enough light to read or sew by. Indeed, nothing much had changed at the farm since Victorian times. Dragon Fell was a bubble in time and the outside world did not much intrude. The situation was too isolated for many folks to bother with, and Alfred did not much care for the current world, so he made no changes. Anna took a lamp and moved to the window to see if she could see her father or the old man as she called him. She was too agitated to read as she was worried that Alfred, her father, had fallen in a snowdrift. The path to the farm was covered in snow. After landing at the airport Alfred would get the bus or hitch as far as he could and then walk up the steep path from the village. He knew it well, but the night was wicked and even he could lose his footing. The clock ticked on, and hours passed. Still no Alfred. Anna was still in her coat as the house was cold at this time of year even with the fires lit. The weather seeped into the stones. The damp could creep into your very bones. The dragon breathed in secret on Anna and kept her well. She curled up on the old sofa and stroked the cat who nestled on her chest.

Just as Anna was drifting to sleep the door banged.

"Oh my God what a night. But I am home at last," said Alfred as he collapsed into the armchair opposite Philip.

His son roused from slumber and got up to embrace Alfred in a bear hug. He leaped back in fright as something sprang out from under Alfred's greatcoat. The creature seemed at first to Philip like an Orc or a goblin in the shadows of the house. Anna had started to move to embrace her father but stepped back on seeing the apparition. On recovering her senses, she realized the dark thing was in fact nothing but a half-starved child. He was about Anna's age but smaller than her with thick almost black hair and thicker brows. His skin was as brown as a shiny conker, but his arms protruded from his body like sticks. The startled child, sensing danger, started speaking loudly in a language nobody could understand and gesturing wildly with his hands. His brown eyes were filled with fear and anger as he struggled to make sense of his new surroundings. Pearl dropped the plate she was carrying, and it smashed into a thousand pieces on the stone floor.

"Now then, now then," said Alfred, "there's no need for all this racket. This is Raven. Well, that's what I've called him anyway. Nobody knows his real name or where he comes from. I found him wandering in the street in Newcastle. I suppose I should take him to the police, but I don't like those children's homes and things I hear about them. Maybe we should just keep him a while. I'll say he's mine. Can you keep a secret do you think?"

Philip looked horrified by this prospect, but he knew better than to anger the old man. He meekly acquiesced and hugged his father with genuine affection. Anna was over her initial fear and stepped up to do the same.

"Yes, Da. Of course, we will keep him. That would be the kind thing to do, poor mite," said Anna.

"I suppose we will. I could do with some more help on the farm anyway," said Philip.

"Champion," said Alfred, "we'll see Raven all right. He's a strong lad and the farm will suit him fine. Nobody needs to know where he came from and if anyone asks to tell them to mind their own business. There are enough nosey parkers in the village. They make up stories about you anyway if they don't know the truth."

Anna stayed at her father's feet as he ate his stew in the chair. Raven calm now that he realized nobody was going to hurt him looked longingly at the stew. Pearl, with more sense than any of them, took Raven by the hand and led him to the table. She set a bowl of stew in front of him and a slice of bread. Raven ate quickly with his hands stuffing everything into his mouth and then draining the bowl like a cup. Pearl laughed at his ill manners even worse than hers. She had learned to be more ladylike since she had come to Dragon Fell.

Anna stood in front of Raven staring at him as if he was an alien fallen from the sky. Never had she seen someone so fierce looking. His mouth snarled as if he did not know how to smile. Tentatively, she smiled at him and put out her hand. Raven reached for it, feeling the fingers as if in amazement. Anna tried to figure out the origins of Raven in her mind. There were only white people in Odinsdale at that time, but Anna had seen pictures of other races in her schoolbooks. It seemed that Indian might be the closest match to him. He had the same skin tone and hair though Raven's was perhaps a little too curly. His face was fine featured with a prominent, narrow nose and thin lips. Anna toyed with the idea that he might be a Romany gypsy. She had seen them at the travelling fair one summer, but Raven's features seemed finer than theirs. He was a mystery.

Alfred roused himself from his armchair and stood up to go to bed.

"Didn't you buy anything for us, Da?" said Anna.

"Ha! What do you think Raven is?" Alfred said, "He's better than any present. A whole new brother to play with."

Anna screwed up her face with disgust. She would have preferred a new doll or a book than this strange child.

"I suppose," she said uncertainly.

"There are no spare beds made up so you better pop him in with Philip. I'm off to sleep. I am fit to collapse," said Alfred.

Now it was Philip's turn to look aghast but there was nothing he could do. Alfred departed leaving the children staring at their new brother. Anna started rudely making faces at Raven now that her father was not there to see her bad behaviour.

"By you are a fierce one," said Anna, poking Raven in the ribs.

Raven's response was to grab Anna by the hair and start raining blows down on her head. Philip jumped in to protect his sister and soon the room seemed a mess of fighting bodies. Pearl saved the day by swinging at Raven with a kitchen pan and soon dragged him away with her. Thinking that bedding down with Philip was not the best idea she put him in her own bed in her tiny room in the roof space of the house. You had to climb up to the attic room with a ladder. Pearl washed Raven's face with a flannel and the water from a bowl. Then she motioned him to get undressed, but he would have none of it. The most she could manage was to get him to remove his boots. Raven snuggled down into the bed looking like he was in Heaven and was soon fast asleep. Pearl, having nowhere else to go, crept in beside him and the two kept each other warm through the night. There was no sound but the owls hooting and the wind blowing steadily. All was black outside and in.

"You'll be all right now Raven," said Pearl, "we'll look after you. You're safe now. I'll be your ma."

Anna and Philip also took themselves to bed on the first floor in their separate bedrooms. Anna just crawled under her covers without removing her coat because it was so cold at night. Her bed was covered with a thick quilt and several blankets. Her room was sparsely furnished with a dark, polished wood wardrobe and a chest of drawers. There were some dolls and board games piled in the corner. The wind whistled down the chimney and rattled the windowpanes. Philip donned some thick pajamas to keep him warm. He had the foresight to light the paraffin heater in his room, so he had heat through the night. He had become used to the metallic smell it emitted. The dogs slept with Philip at the foot of the bed, curling around each other so you could not tell where one dog ended and the other began.

Alfred was snoring loudly in his bedroom, glad to have rest after all his hard work. His dreams were full of his long dead wife, Joanie. In his visions they were both young again, walking in the fields or cutting the hay at harvest time. Joanie was offering him a cup of cider and he kissed her with abandon. It was always summer in Alfred's dreams and Joanie was always smiling.

The storm blew itself out and silence fell upon the Dale. The stars were hidden behind the bank of cloud as the night creatures went about their business. The barn owls were on the hunt and Old Broc was abroad looking for food. The shaggy old fox was trying to find a way into the hen house to cause the bloodbath he craved in his heart. Mice slunk into the house to see what scraps they could find. In the barn, rats scuffled in the straw as Stanley dozed standing up. All slept soundly at Dragon Fell Farm.

Chapter Two

Dawn broke to find Raven sitting at the kitchen table being taught by Pearl to eat porridge with a spoon. He looked around himself with amazement. Everything was strange and foreign to him. The stone flags were swept clean by Pearl and the copper pans shone on their hooks. High in the eaves hams and legs of lamb were hanging from the roof beams. The old high-backed chairs by the fire were made more comfortable with sheepskins draped over them. There was a delicious smell of baking bread wafting through the air and a pile of oatcakes on the kitchen counter. Raven smiled at Pearl. He had not known kindness in his life so far. The porridge was warming his insides and filling his belly. This was good. Pearl, happy to have a new companion, pointed out things in the room and named them in the hopes of teaching Raven English. The child learned fast and repeated the names after Pearl. It dawned on him that he too had a name.

"I am Raven," he said, smiling at Pearl. Pearl clapped her hands for joy and held his face in her hands. She could see he was intelligent with much promise. It was like having a child of her own, something she had secretly longed for in her heart.

Anna arrived at the table and wolfed down her porridge. She eyed Raven warily. Should she make an enemy of him or a friend? She decided on friend. Anna had never had a friend. Philip was too old to be a playmate. Her friends were her pets, the farm animals and creatures she found on the moor. She had never been to school. Alfred pretended he home-schooled her, but he just gave her books to read and maths booklets to fill in. Anna found the work easy and completed her daily tasks within an hour. Then she was free to do as she pleased.

"Would you like to see the farm?" she said to Raven.

She realised he couldn't understand. She put on her coat and found an old one of

Philip's hanging on a peg. Pearl showed Raven how to wear it and he stood proudly, pleased with himself.

Anna and Raven ran out into the yard. It was a cold but fine day with the sun just rising over the hill. The pair ran out on to the moor to enjoy the day. The snow was still deep, but Anna knew how to avoid the most treacherous parts and find paths through. The world was silent other than the crunching of the snow under the children's boots. They tramped to the top of the hill and then took in the view. Anna pointed out the landmarks to her companion. There were two reservoirs and a few small farms with stone barns for the sheep. Odinsdale Hall stood in the distance, home of the Fitzwilliam family, right down in the valley where there was no snow even today. It was surrounded by walls, metal railings and trees, protected from the worst of the weather. Anna had never walked there but she wondered about it often and who would live in such a grand house. There was a road in the distance, but no cars were travelling on it on such a day as this.

"This is Odinsdale," said Anna, "We are the highest farm. And the best one. We have two hundred sheep and twenty cattle. We are kings of all we survey."

She let out a scream into the wind and Raven copied her. Their voices were carried away and nobody could hear them. They screamed and screamed until they felt exhausted.

Anna took Raven's hand, and they ran down the hill. They paused to make a snow man, using twigs for his arms and nose. Then they threw snowballs at each other, collapsing into giggles on the hard ground. Anna showed Raven how to make snow angels, laying on the earth and moving her hands up and down. They admired their handiwork. The wind blew incessantly as a barn owl flew over the children's heads like a ghost from another world. A flock of goldfinches were feeding on thistle heads, their song a charm, weaving a spell on the land.

The pair eventually returned to the farm. Anna took Raven into the barn and introduced Raven to Stanley. His eyes lit up at the sight of the pony.

"Stanley," said Anna slowly, pointing at the beast.

"Stanley," repeated Raven confidently.

"Yes, Yes. Well done. He's my pony. I'll show you how to groom him," said Anna.

She gave Raven a dandy brush and they both set about grooming Stanley until his coat was as clean as could be. Then Anna showed Raven how to pick out the dirt from his hooves with a hoof pick. She placed a bridle on Stanley, and they went out into the yard. It was too snowy to go far today so Anna walked the pony round the yard.

"Would you like to ride him?" Anna asked Raven.

Raven didn't understand. Anna mimed getting on Stanley and he nodded excitedly.

Anna took the pony to the mounting block and helped Raven on to Stanley. Anna led Stanley around in a circle.

Raven sat up tall, proud of his achievement. Anna increased the pony's pace to a trot and Raven bobbed up and down but managed to remain seated.

"Well done Raven. You are a natural," Anna said.

Raven beamed in delight. Anna took Stanley back into the barn and fed him some hay and a scoop of oats. As the pair left the barn the snow started again. They went back inside the house.

They pulled off their boots and warmed their feet in front of the range. Pearl fed them some beef stew and fresh bread. Raven worked his teeth hard on the gristly meat. Anna playfully chastised him for the noises he was making, and he tried to eat more quietly. After their meal, which Pearl called dinner even though it was the middle of the day, the children settled down in front of the fire looking at some of Anna's old picture books so Raven could learn to read. Anna pointed at things and said the English word. Raven repeated after Anna. Then Anna taught him some nursery rhymes.

They finished the afternoon with Anna reading Raven a Beatrix Potter story about Peter Rabbit. Anna put on silly voices for the characters and Raven roared with laughter. Pretty soon it was time for what Pearl called tea. They had sausages and chips at the kitchen table with apple crumble for dessert. After tea they played a game of drafts with Anna teaching raven the rules. Pearl came to put them to bed.

"Time for bed, you two," she said.

"No Pearl. We're having too much fun. We want to stay up late," said Anna.

"Now Anna, don't be cheeky," said Pearl.

Anna threw her book across the room in temper.

"That's enough Anna. Get to bed," said Alfred from his place by the fire where he was sucking contentedly on a pipe and gazing into the flames.

Anna took Raven by the hand, and they went upstairs. Anna decided Raven should bunk in with her instead of Pearl.

She fetched a mattress from the junk room and made it up for Raven on the floor with plenty of blankets. Raven snuggled down in it contentedly and promptly fell asleep. Anna crawled into her own bed and did the same. She sighed happily. It had been such a good day and she had made a real friend.

The following morning Alfred set Raven to work clearing the path with a shovel. Raven worked hard all morning moving the snow on to the grass so people could walk down the path with ease. Alfred came out to check on him from time to time and was pleased with his diligence. After dinner, which was at lunch time, Alfred showed Raven how to muck out the stable and take the dung to the manure heap. The boy worked hard at the task, barely stopping for breath.

"Raven, tha's a good lad. You've worked hard this morning. We'll make a Yorkshireman of you yet," said Alfred with a laugh.

He gave Raven a shiny penny in thanks for his labour.

Anna came running out to see what was happening.

"Have you finished with Raven? I want him to see the moor," said Anna.

"Yes. Why don't you take him up to the reservoir? The light is pretty on the water at this time of year."

"Good idea Da," said Anna.

She took Raven by the hand, and they set off across the moor. The snow was deep, but Anna knew how to get through. She knew every inch of the moor near the farm. After a long walk they ended up at the new reservoir. It was a large expanse of water surrounded by bare, black trees. Nobody else was around. The crow's acked acked to each other from the branches. There was thick ice where the water should have been. They slid out on to the ice, laughing together. They moved their feet as if they were wearing skates and danced around with each other. At one point, some of the ice broke near Anna and she fell in. The water was icy cold, and Anna waved her arms around screaming for help. Raven knew what to do instinctively. He laid down on the ice so that his weight was spread evenly. Then he crawled towards the hole. Once within reach of Anna Raven hauled her out with ease. He carried her away from the ice and set her down on the snow. Anna's teeth were chattering, and she was as pale as the snow she sat on. She hugged Raven tightly.

"Oh, Raven you saved me. You are my hero," said Anna.

"Raven is...strong," said Raven, testing out his newly learned English speech.

"Very strong. And brave. We are going to be a great team, you and I," said Anna.

After that they decided to return home before any more disasters befell them.

***

As time passed, Raven and Anna became inseparable. It was as if a cord joined their two souls together and could not be broken. They both grew tall and strong, held up by fresh air and simple plain food. Philip was wary of Raven and kept to himself, working the farm and going to bed at dusk. He lived much like one of the animals of the moor, contented with his own company. Alfred was well pleased with Raven and made him a favourite. The child was quiet and even tempered, not as spirited as Anna nor as likely to make cheeky remarks. Alfred thought Raven's calm demeanour meant he had a good heart but there was a dark side to him that became apparent to Anna even in childhood.

***

One time when the children were just ten they were riding their ponies into the village. They both had hardy black Fell ponies with quiet temperaments. They cantered over the moors making it a race between them. Anna won of course. Raven always let her win. They came to the path that led down to the road travelling in single file now. Eventually they reached the road and trotted along. Anna spied a rabbit that had been injured by the roadside. He was quivering and jerking, not yet dead. He must have been hit by a car. Anna dismounted and rushed towards the creature with concern. Raven laughed at the misfortune of the rabbit and swung his legs over his pony's back to reach the ground.

"Raven don't laugh. He's hurting. How can you do that?"

"It's just a rabbit, Anna."

In one swift movement, he lunged forward and decapitated the animal with his pocketknife. Then he stood smiling, proud of his act. Anna turned and thumped him on the chest with her fist.

"Raven, you are wicked, wicked," she said as she scooped up the pieces of rabbit and headed to the verge to bury it.

Raven, crestfallen that he had hurt Anna's feelings, helped to dig a grave and laid the rabbit in it. Anna made a cross out of two pieces of twig and said a prayer over the burial mound.

"Dear God, Help this rabbit to go to Heaven where it can play with its brothers and sisters. Forgive Raven his sins. Amen."

They rode on to the village in silence. Anna occasionally turned to Raven to frown at him. Forgiveness did not come easily to her. Once they arrived at the village store Raven bought sweets for them both with his pocket money. They sucked on huge gobstoppers as they made their way home. It was a warm spring day, and the daffodils were bobbing in the breeze on the village green. A stream ran through the centre of the village and the water babbled comfortingly as they rode by. Anna's mood was much improved by the sweets as she enjoyed the beauty of the surroundings.

As they were riding along the track they noticed a group of children standing at the side watching them.

"Hello," said one of the girls, "Who might you be?"

"I'm Anna and this is Raven. We're from Dragon Fell Farm," said Anna.

"My you do look a queer pair," said one of the boys, "Where do you buy your clothes, Oxfam?"

“Shut up. You can’t speak to us like that,” said Raven.

“Gonna make me,” said the boy.

Raven dismounted and took a punch at the boy who had spoken. He felled him with one blow. Raven spat on him as he was on the ground. The other children ran off in terror, shocked by the quick violence and the strength which Raven had shown and skill in fighting.

“Just leave him Raven. Come on. We need to get back,” said Anna, “You shouldn’t fight with people. It will get you in trouble. You must learn to control yourself.”

“Why shouldn’t I have hit him? He had it coming. You can’t just let people insult you Anna,” said her play mate.

Raven kicked the boy as he lay there and then mounted his pony. They cantered off together back to the farm. Anna knew better than to tell anyone about the incident. She worried that the boy’s parents would come up to the house, but nothing happened.

***

Anna's heart was still troubled by the darkness in Raven. She noticed this more and more as he grew older. He would stamp on insects and small creatures, pull the wings off flies, tear butterflies to shreds and kill an injured bird rather than try to save it. He learned to shoot with the shotgun and killed the rabbits and rats around the farm with pleasure. Sometimes, he managed to shoot a fox. Anna found she could only stop him by telling him that it displeased her. For her he would do good acts, not for himself.

***

One summer Raven and Anna persuaded Pearl to give them a picnic and set off for the moors. They had jam sandwiches, a pork pie each and a slab of Wensleydale cheese. There was even a bottle of lemonade for them to drink – a rare treat. Anna was a strong girl of twelve now. Who knows how old Raven was but probably about the same? They walked and walked until they reached the little waterfall that fell into a pool. The smooth rocks around it made a good place to stop and eat. Anna spread out the cloth she had brought and laid out the feast. They ate with gusto and then laid down on the cloth to soak up the sun. It was a rare, sunny clear day. Hay making had finished and life was easy now on the farm.

"What do you want to be when you grow up?" said Anna.

"I will work the farm and buy up all the land around. I will be the biggest and richest farmer in all of Yorkshire."

"That sounds good. But what about Philip? He will inherit the farm."

"No, he will pick a fight in The Red Lion and a travelling labourer will kill him. Then the farm will pass to me."

"Raven. It's wicked to wish death on someone. You mustn't think such things."

"Why? Who says it's wicked?'

"God says."

"How do you know what God thinks? You never go to church."

"That isn't the point. I know right from wrong. I read the Bible."

"Well, I don't know much about God. But I know nature. Look around. The buzzards kill the mice. The foxes kill the hens. The birds kill the worms. This is the way of things. The strong win. The weak die. I'm going to be strong."

"That doesn't seem right to me. I'm not an animal. I'm a person. So are you. We have souls. We must do right in the world."

Raven snorted in disgust at Anna's words. He leaned over and kissed her on the cheek.

"I'm going to marry you, Anna," Raven said.

Anna laughed. Raven sat on her chest, bestriding her. He kissed her full on the mouth. Anna felt his urgency and the pressure of his mouth.

"No. Don't do that Raven," she screamed and beat her fists on him.

He rolled off and stared at the sky.

"We can't get married. We're like brother and sister. We'll always be together but not like that."

"I don't see why not. We're not related. Alfred found me remember," said Raven.

"But we're family. It's not right."

"Course it is. You'll see. There's nobody better than me in the Dale."

They got up and walked along the path in silence. Anna admired the heather in bloom that had turned the moor purple. They walked back to the farm hand in hand.

***

As the years passed Raven and Anna grew closer and closer. Their days took a familiar pattern. Anna did her schoolwork and rode her pony. Raven did a little schooling but mostly he worked on the farm with Philip. All his spare time was spent with Anna. They were happy in their rough-hewn bubble.

***

The year Anna turned fifteen the summer was glorious. It was hotter and drier than usual on the moor. Anna was sunbathing in the garden behind the house. She didn't have a bikini, so she rucked up her summer dress to show off her legs to the sun. She wanted to be brown like the women in the magazines she sometimes read. Alfred was away working. Anna took full advantage and lazed away the summer. Raven appeared around the corner of the house covered in bits from hay making. He laid down next to Anna. They held hands like good companions as the sun beat down on their unaccustomed white flesh.

"Don't you just love summer?" asked Anna.

"Yes. The insects buzzing, the butterflies, the flowers. Everything is alive, growing and changing," said Raven.

"We are growing and changing too. I am almost grown up now. I am a lady."

Raven laughed at this idea.

"We aren't lords and ladies. We're good honest folk. We work for our bread. That's how it should be. I love working on the land. Watching things grow. Tending the beasts. It's how things should be."

"But it would be fun to be a lady. Like in an old book. I would like to go to parties and wear a ball gown. Sip champagne."

Raven leaned over and pecked her on the cheek. Anna moved away slightly, wary of his tendency to too strong affection.

"I'll take you to a ball one day Anna. Just you see if I don't."

"We'll have to get rich first."

"I'm working on that."

Pearl appeared with a tray of home-made lemonade and cake. They all sat together eating and drinking with good cheer. Anna made a daisy chain and wrapped it round Pearl's wrist.

"Now you are Queen of the Fairies," Anna announced.

Raven had to go one better and gathered a posy of wildflowers from the bottom of the garden and gave them to Anna. The girl clutched them to her breast breathing in the scent. The sun continued to blaze as they dozed in the light.

"I like the sun," said Pearl. "Who made the sun do you think?"

"Well God of course," said Anna.

"Scientists say it's just an accident. A big bang happened, and everything came into being. All the planets and stars and the sun. One day it will stop burning and everything will die," said Raven.

"I don't believe that. Scientists don't know what they're talking about. How can they possibly know? They weren't there at the beginning. They just like puffing themselves up and feeling important. They make money out of pretending to know things. I just feel in my bones that God made it. I just know. He wouldn't let it be destroyed. Life goes on forever. There are seasons and times and rhythms and then it all starts again," said Anna.

"I like Anna's version best," said Pearl.

"Aha, it's two against one, you're beaten," said Anna and began beating Raven playfully on the chest. They continued play fighting and rolled down the bank to the bottom of the garden.

***

That summer the travelling fair came to the village. The gypsies pitched camp about half a mile from the settlement. There were caravans and fairground rides. The air was filled with the sound of an elephant trumpeting and the roar of lions. A big wheel with chairs attached dominated the skyline. Loud pop music was blaring out from loudspeakers.

Raven saw it from the hill as he was mending a stone wall on the moor. He went back to the farm for dinner full of his news.

"Guess what? There is a fair at the village. I saw it. We should go. It will be fun."

"Maybe. We don't have any money to go," said Anna.

"I've got a little money put by," said Pearl, "we could use that. I've never been to a fair."

"That's settled then. We'll go tomorrow after tea," said Raven.

The appointed time arrived, and Raven, Pearl and Anna put on their best clothes. Raven was in his smart jeans and a checked shirt. Anna was wearing a flower print summer dress and Pearl had a plaid skirt and shirt on. The evening was warm, and they grew tired and sweaty walking towards the fair. On arrival, Pearl bought everyone a can of cola. They enjoyed the treat, swallowing the sweet liquid quickly. They didn't normally have such a luxury. They made do with water and tea at the farm. After they had refreshed themselves they walked round the fair, taking everything in. The melange of sounds and strange sights made Pearl feel queasy. She was used to the quiet of the moor. She saw a stall selling ice cream and bought everyone one. Raven had chocolate while Anna chose strawberry. Pearl, cautious by nature, settled for vanilla. They walked on, enjoying the sweet taste. They stopped in front of the big wheel in awe.

"We must go on this. It's amazing. We'll be able to see all over the Dale," said Raven.

"Yes. Let's do it. Come on," said Anna.

"No, no. I feel a bit sick already. You go. I'll just have a walk round," said Pearl.

Anna and Raven paid their money to the large scruffy man in charge and sat in one of the chairs with the bar pulled across. They were laughing and their faces shone with excitement.

Pearl waved at them and then meandered around the stalls. While admiring a boy's skill at the coconut shy a young man made a bee line for her.

"Well, well, young lady, who might you be?" said the man.

"I'm Pearl from Dragon Fell Farm," said Pearl.

"They call me Tony. I'm down from Durham visiting some friends," said Tony.

He gazed longingly at Pearl like an eagle looking at his prey.

"I'll buy you a beer, what do you say?" said Tony.

Pearl felt unsure but she agreed. She was still thirsty after the long walk here and she liked beer on the odd occasion she had tried it. They walked to the beer tent and Pearl received her beer in a plastic glass. She sipped at it shyly.

"Let's find somewhere quiet to sit," said Tony.

They walked away from the fair across the field and finally sat down under the shade of some trees.

"So, what do you do at Dragon Fell Farm then?" said Tony.

"I'm a general assistant. I do a bit of everything. I look after the children and clean and cook."

"Do you like it?"

"Yes. Everyone is kind to me. It's a great place. I'm like family."

"Do you have a husband or a boyfriend?"

"No. I don't really meet anyone. The farm is quite alone, and I don't get out much. There's always too much to do. Anyway, I've never been popular with the local lads. They never liked me at school."

"I like you. I sell cars in Durham. I'm very successful."

With that he kissed her forcefully on the lips. Pearl felt herself melting into him. She didn't know what to do. She had never been kissed before by a man. His breath smelled of beer. Before she knew it, she was lying on her back on the ground with Tony on top of her. He was pulling up her skirt and then she felt him pulling at her tights. Pearl recoiled in terror as she had some inkling about what was happening. She fought him off with all her might. All that housework at the farm had given her strong arms. He tried to pin her down, but she managed to get one of her fists free and punched him full on the nose. Bleeding, he stood up and she ran away back to the fair.

Pearl was shaking in shock, but she found the toilet block and went in. She splashed water on her face and adjusted her skirt and blouse. She smiled at her reflection in the mirror, trying to look normal for when she returned to Anna and Raven. She decided not to say anything. She had a lucky escape. She felt like she had let the children down. She walked back towards the big wheel where Anna and Raven were already waiting for her.

"Pearl, where have you been? We were getting worried about you. You look so pale. What on earth has happened?" said Anna.

"It's nothing. I just feel a bit queasy is all. I'll be all right in a bit," said Pearl.

Anna hugged her tightly, looking at her with concern.

"We must go back to Dragon Fell. You can lie down and recover. Maybe the excitement is all too much," said Anna.

"No, there is so much we haven't seen. Pearl will be all right, won't you Pearl?" said Raven.

"Yes, I'll be fine," said Pearl.

"Raven no, we must go back at once. You are so unfeeling. You must think about others," said Anna.

"Can we just go and look at the elephants?" asked Raven.

"I guess that might be all right," said Anna.

She hooked arms with Pearl, and they went off to the elephant enclosure. There were two large elephants eating hay. They were attached to a post with chains. They looked old and wrinkly, and their eyes were rheumy.

"They don't look happy," said Anna, "I am sure they don't need to chain them. It seems so cruel."

She pushed her fingers through the mesh, but the animal did not look towards her.

"Let's just go then," said Raven, disappointed in the mangy look of the elephants.

They walked back up the hill to the farm with Raven giving Pearl a piggyback at the rough parts as she still seemed unsteady. Eventually, they arrived back at Dragon Fell and Anna tucked Pearl up in bed and made her some sweet tea. Raven went out to tend to the beasts.

"Are you sure you are ok. Pearl? Did anything happen when we were on the big wheel? You can tell me," said Anna.

"No, no. I think I've just had a funny turn. Don't worry about me Anna. I'm fine. You're so kind. It's wonderful how you've grown up. And you have such a good effect on Raven. He always behaves better when you're there," said Pearl.

Anna patted her head and then held Pearl's hand until she fell into a deep sleep.

***

Summer turned to Autumn and the wind became colder. Harvest was finished and everything was gathered for the winter. The beasts had plenty of hay for their forage over the cold months stacked in bales in the barn. There were also sacks of oats and barley and plenty of straw for bedding. Pearl had spent many hours canning and preserving the produce. She made piccalilli, raspberry jam, tomato chutney, and onion relish. The kitchen shelves were lined with jars. There were sacks of potatoes in the back of the kitchen and plenty of oatmeal to see them all through. Tired of kitchen work Pearl took it into her head to go down to the road to see if there was any post. She put on her wellingtons, coat, and woollen bunnet and set off. The afternoon was bright with a keen wind, but Pearl was glad to be out in the open. She sang an old tune as she walked and admired the little rumps of the rabbits scattering in front of her. Eventually she arrived at the box by the roadside and fished out the post. There were several letters but one looked thick and important. Pearl could barely read so she didn't know where it was from. She rested for a while and then set off back up the hill. On arrival at the gate, she saw Philip coming in from the fields. She gave him the letters and busied herself making tea.

Philip took off his boots and sat by the fire. He picked up the thick letter which was addressed to him. As he read his face became whiter and whiter.
"What's wrong?" said Pearl.

Philip eyes were wild. He shouted up the stairs, "Raven, Anna, get down here!"

Anna and Raven came clattering down the stairs like young deer. On seeing

Philip's face, they came to a halt in front of him.

"You all better sit down," said Philip.

"I got this letter from the oil company. Da is dead. There was an accident on the rig. A fire broke out in the accommodation block. They all burned to death. There is no body. Oh my God."

Pearl, Anna and Raven stood in shock. Anna rushed to hug Philip and Pearl joined in. Raven stood to the side not saying anything or moving at all. A rock. They passed the evening staring into the fire saying little. Anna found tears continually falling from her eyes. Raven comforted her with his arm around her. Philip kept tapping the chair arm with his fingers, his mind turning over and over. It was almost impossible to process. Da had been a part of the farm forever. Even though he worked away a lot he had been a steadying force, guiding them all through the trials of life. Dragon Fell Farm without Alfred was unthinkable. Philip did not feel ready to take the reins. He had assumed this day would be a long time in the future.

After a time, Anna and Raven crept up to bed. They bunked in together, hugging each other. Anna cried uncontrollably and was grateful for the warmth of Raven's body.

"It's all right, Anna," said Raven, "I'll always look after you. We'll always be together you and me. We have the farm, and each other.

"I know Raven. I'm so grateful for you. It was a fateful day when you arrived here. I think you were sent to be with me," said Anna and kissed Raven's cheek.

Philip went into town later in the week to see the solicitor. It turned out he had inherited everything, lock, stock and barrel. Anna was awarded some jewellery which had been her mother's and a small sum of money. Raven also received a few thousand pounds. When Philip returned and told them of his good fortune Raven's face turned red. He left without a word, mounted his pony and galloped him mercilessly for hours over the moors. He returned late at night, the poor horse exhausted and foaming at the mouth. Raven had hoped for a share in the farm, at least some of it but it was not to be. He crawled into bed beside Anna muttering about his revenge.

"I'm gonna see to him, that cunt. I'm taking the farm from him; you see if I don't. Dragon Fell belongs to me."

Anna stroked his hair and made comforting noises.

"Now then, Raven, don't take on so. Everything will be all right. We're all still together. That's what matters."

Raven shook his head. His body was rigid with anger. Anna had a feeling of foreboding. Everything had changed. Their carefree childhood was gone. The world seemed dark and forbidding. She couldn't sleep that night and just stared into space. Raven slept fitfully, swearing and moaning through the night.

The following morning at breakfast the little family were at the kitchen table having their porridge. Philip was pleased with himself, laying out plans for the farm.

"We need to diversify. Grow more things. Maybe even let tourists camp in one of the fields. I've got ideas. We need to make it pay more. Raven you can work for me. Bed and board. I can't spare much else. Maybe a couple of pounds a week. Anna, I'll look after you. Give you some pocket money. Maybe you should start looking for a husband."

Raven glowered but grunted his assent. Anna said nothing but just played with her porridge.

"What about me?" said Pearl as she brought in the teapot?

"You can stay on just the same Pearl. You do a great job here so I would be glad for you to stay," said Philip.

"Thank you, Philip. That's kind of you. I should be glad to stay on," said Pearl.

"Champion. Champion. Things are going to be great. There's no need for these long faces. Life goes on," said Philip, chuckling to himself.

***

At first, things seemed to go along well. The farm had its rhythms. Despite his grand talk Philip did not change very much at Dragon Fell. It had a way of carrying on with its old ways. There was so much to do on the farm that Philip was dog tired most of the time. Sadly, power went to his head, and he became tyrannical towards the others. He had none of the geniality and kind nature of his father.

***

One lunch time he swaggered into the house as usual.

"Where's my dinner, Pearl?" he roared.

Pearl, flustered by his tone, rushed to the range and started doling out the soup she had made. She brought it to him and laid it in front of him with some thick slices of home-made bread.

She placed bowls in the other places and called the others.

"Anna, Raven, your dinner's ready."

Anna and Raven rushed in, giggling and flushed red from the game they had been playing.

"You two, get your dinner and stop acting the goat," commanded Philip.

"Yes, sir," said Raven with a disrespectful smirk.

Philip responded by hitting him so hard across the face that Raven fell of his chair. He hit the stone flags hard and bruised his face. Breathing heavily, Raven said not a word. He got up, dusted himself off and went out to his farm work. He never spoke a word to Philip again other than to grunt his assent to work instructions.

Anna and Pearl were too stunned to say anything. Pearl was nervous by nature and now she was worried about losing her place. She needed the money to look after her mother. She would not admonish Philip for his behaviour. Anna was confused. She had had no idea what hatred Philip had harboured in his heart for Raven. Now it was obvious. She had no idea what to do. Anna worried she might be turfed out. She knew nothing of the world, and it frightened her. Living in so isolated a place she had never been invited to anything in the neighbourhood and she knew nobody. She had read enough romance novels to dream of a perfect husband, but she didn't know how to go about it. In books people were invited to balls and parties. They were courted by glamourous gentlemen of the neighbourhood. She had no money to her name, and she would not inherit the farm. No hopefuls would come calling. She wanted to stay with Raven, but his position was becoming worse and worse. If only they had enough money to escape but they didn't. Anna needed a place to live and some income. She had neither. How was she to catch a husband in the lonely Dale? She didn't dare to say anything to Philip about his treatment of Raven, but she worried in her heart. At night the protective fire dragon breathed her love on her and comforted her mind. Anna prayed to God for a way out.

***

A gloom descended on Dragon Fell. Raven went about his farm work with a sullen expression. He took his meagre wages and saved them in a box under his bed. He plotted insane schemes in his mind. He thought of murdering Philip in his bed and hiding the body. One night he brought a heavy hammer in from the barn and hid it under his mattress. Night fell and he pretended to sleep. In the early hours Raven crept into Philip's room with the hammer. Owls were hooting around the farm and the moonlight lit up the room. He went up to the bed and saw Philip happily sleeping there. He raised the hammer above his head. Something stopped him at that moment. He thought of Anna. What if he didn't get away with it? If he went to prison Anna would have nobody to look after her. He put his hand back down at his side and returned to bed. He still wanted revenge, but he had to be more subtle.

There must be a way. All Raven wanted in the world was to marry Anna and give her everything she wanted. His fitful sleep was full of Anna: Anna walking through fields of wildflowers; Anna galloping across the moor; Anna in a bridal gown marrying Raven; Anna and Raven surrounded by their adoring children, the proud owners of Dragon Fell Farm. There had to be a plan if he could only think of it.

Chapter Three

August came and the sun blazed down on Odinsdale. Such a perfect day was a rare thing. Philip was away buying farm machinery in the local market town. Pearl was busy scrubbing the kitchen floor. Anna flung her maths booklet across the room.

"Bugger this. Let's go riding," Anna said.

"Definitely. It's too good a day to waste on schoolwork," said Raven, who had taken the day off to be with Anna as he knew Philip wasn't around.

They ran to the stable and put bridles on the Fell ponies. They didn't have saddles but just perched bareback. Years of practice had given them strong seats. Anna was wearing some old, patched jeans and no shoes. Raven had rubber wellingtons and army surplus trousers. Neither of them gave much thought to how they looked. Anna's wild, red hair was twisted into plaits from which it was constantly trying to escape. They cantered across the moor, bare headed and jumped some low fences to reach the tops. Anna laughed with delight as they slowed to admire the view below them. She screamed into the wind with all her might. Raven joined her, howling like a wolf.

As they descended on the other side of the hill they spied a lone horseman coming the other way.

"Who on earth is that?" said Anna.

"Let's find out. Race you," said Raven.

They galloped towards the figure and pulled up close to the lone man. Raven raised his hand in greeting taking in the slight young man riding a very fine horse that looked like a thoroughbred. The youth looked startled at the two rough-hewn riders who had unexpectedly crossed his path.

"Hello," said Anna looking at him with her intense eyes as if she could see right through him.

"Hello," the man replied. "To whom do I have the pleasure of speaking? It's rare I meet anyone out on these hills. I'm Rupert Fitzwilliam. I live at Odinsdale Hall. I'm just back from boarding school."

Anna laughed, amazed at his way of speaking. He had such a gentle tone and long vowels. She had never heard anyone speak like that before.

"I'm Anna, This is Raven. We're from Dragon Fell Farm."

She pointed to show where they had come from. Raven didn't smile as he regarded the youth with some unease.

"Dragon Fell. I have heard my father talk of it," said Rupert. "It must be cold there in winter. We are a bit milder at the Hall, being lower down."

Anna smiled more broadly. Rupert seemed like a fairy tale character to her. He was tall and thin with blonde hair and fine features. He looked like the prince in the Cinderella book she had read as a child. Anna felt something stir within her, like her insides were contracting.

"Shall we ride together?" said Anna.

Rupert nodded his assent, and the three riders descended the hill. Rupert pointed out landmarks and features of the landscape, showing himself knowledgeable and thoughtful. He drew Anna's attention to the swallows flying low across the moorlands. He shared his binoculars with her so she could get a good look at the red grouse in the distance. Rupert informed Anna that the bird calling was a golden plover. The moors were alive with the sound of grasshoppers and crickets. Nature was at play. Anna felt totally relaxed in his company, allowing her heart to sing. She felt sunshine pour into her. Raven brought up the rear, head bowed and with a sullen expression on his face. Rupert pointedly ignored him while addressing all his remarks to Anna.

"So, what are you doing now you are back from school?" said Anna.

"Well, I am learning to run the estate. One day I will take over from my father you know. We also have a small racehorse stud. I want to develop that more. If we got the right staff I think we could make some serious money. Then I have plans for some of our neglected outbuildings. With a bit of work, I think we could turn them into holiday lets. People will pay good money to stay in a place as beautiful as this. Get away from it all. It's so peaceful. I'm glad to be back from school. I'm afraid I wasn't very academic. I like reading though it's just I wasn't good at organising my thoughts on paper. But here I feel at ease. I think I can really make a go of the Hall. Do you know I have a sister? Abigail. I'm afraid she has delicate health. She's in a wheelchair. Something happened at birth. She's never been to school. Just like you. I'm sure you could be great friends. It's a lonely place at times here. Sorry, I'm prattling on."

"Not at all," said Anna, "I like to hear you talk. You have such a soft voice. What's the word? Mellifluous. That's it. So different to how we talk at Dragon Fell. Isn't it beautiful Raven?"

Raven snorted and said nothing about Rupert.

"We are behind the times at Dragon Fell. Do you know there isn't even a road to the farm? We must walk two fields down to the road. All our groceries are dropped off there. We have no electricity or running water. No central heating. I've read about all these things in books and magazines. I bet Odinsdale Hall is a very different place," said Anna.

"Oh yes," said Rupert, "It's very fine. I am so privileged."

"It's time we were getting back now," said Raven, "We have many miles to go back to the farm and the ponies are tired."

"Of course," said Rupert. "But I've so enjoyed meeting you both. You must come to tea. We have a wonderful housekeeper who does the most amazing afternoon teas. Will you come?"

What about Sunday afternoon? Would that suit? About three? I could send a car to meet you at the main road. Then you won't have to walk so far."

"Oh yes, yes," said Anna with joy in her voice. "That would be wonderful. I should like to meet Abigail. Won't it be amazing Raven? We'll wait at the road below the farm at three."

Raven forced a smile in response.

"Brilliant. I shall see you both then," said Rupert and trotted off.

Anna counted down the days until Sunday. What was she to wear? Worried she had nothing suitable Anna went into her mother's old room. She opened the old wardrobe and found several items of clothing. She tried on a flowered pattern dress with a cinched in waist and wide skirt. There was no mirror, but Anna felt she looked good in it. The dress seemed to fit her perfectly. Joanie, Anna's mother, had died many years before. It was a sudden heart attack, just out of the blue with no apparent reason.

"Thanks Mum," whispered Anna to the air.

She took off the dress and stored it carefully in her own wardrobe. Then she went to find Raven.

"Raven what you are wearing on Sunday for the tea?" she said.

"Wearing. I don't know. Just what I always wear," Raven said.

"No. You must look respectable. I'll find something of the old man's. Come and look," Anna said.

Back upstairs they went and rummaged in Alfred's belongings. They tried on all sorts of things together, laughing at each other. Anna donned a flat tweed cap and put a pipe in her mouth. She managed a passable impression of her father. Raven roared with laughter. After much debate, Raven decided on some dark green corduroy trousers, a tweed jacket and brown brogues. He had never felt so smart. Anna hugged him close after admiring his ensemble, drinking in the smell of her father's tobacco.

Sunday finally came. Anna felt agitated all day. Raven went about his farm work as usual. As the sun climbed past noon Anna hauled the tin bath in front of the range. She boiled kettles of hot water to make a bath. She must look her best. She got Pearl to help her scrub herself with soap. Raven came in whistling, and she make him undergo the same procedure. Then they both went upstairs and donned their fine clothes they had picked out. Raven couldn't get his hair to go down flat no matter what he tried. Anna brushed her hair out and it shone like copper. Raven admired her.

"You look beautiful Anna. So fine," said Raven.

"Thanks. You're not so bad yourself," said Anna laughing.

They walked hurriedly down to the road through the fields, trying not to dirty their shoes too much. Arriving at the road they were shocked to find a black Bentley already waiting for them. The driver got out and opened the door for them. They climbed in, admiring the leather seats. The car purred along until it arrived at Odinsdale Hall and swept in through the front gates. The driver opened the door for them, and they went up the steps to the front door nervously. The door opened without them having to ring the bell and an elderly lady welcomed them in.

"I'm Mrs Harbottle, the housekeeper. Rupert is waiting for you in the morning room," the lady said and signalled them to follow her down the hall. Anna and Raven drank everything in with big eyes. There were portraits of various men along the walls and some stags' heads adorned the wooden panelling. Anna's heels clicked as she walked on the black and white tiles.

Mrs Harbottle opened a heavy wooden door, ushered them through and then left. Edgar was sitting in a leather armchair by a roaring fire with a Pekinese dog in his lap. Opposite him was a slender girl in a wheelchair. She had a tartan rug around her legs and a velvet bow in her curly blonde hair. Her skin was paler than anyone Anna had ever seen. Edgar rose as he saw them come in and kissed Anna on both cheeks.

Much to Raven's surprise he did the same to Raven.

"It's so wonderful to see you both. This is my sister Abigail," said Rupert.

Anna rushed to kiss Abigail while Raven just stood awkwardly. Rupert guided them to sit at a nearby table and pushed his sister to her place.

"Do sit down. Tea will arrive shortly," said Edgar.

"I'm absolutely famished," said Abigail.

As if on cue Mrs Harbottle arrived pushing a tray with the tea things which she arranged carefully on the table. There were scones with jam and cream, little cakes and tiny sandwiches with the crusts cut off. Mrs Harbottle poured tea for them all and then left the room. Anna had time to take in her surroundings. The morning room was grander than anything she could have imagined. There was a large chandelier hanging in the centre of the ceiling and the bulbs were lit by electric light. The walls were a light blue with plaster designs of Greek urns and goddesses standing out in white. Paintings in golden frames adorned the lower walls: depictions of cattle, horses and dogs. There was a dark red Persian rug in front of the fireplace and a French clock on the mantlepiece. Large radiators heated the room pleasantly.

Raven was chomping on one of the sandwiches. For the first time Anna noticed his lack of table manners in comparison to Rupert and Abigail. The residents of Odinsdale Hall were nibbling daintily between sips of tea, discussing the weather and current affairs. Raven looked like a dark devil beside Rupert. Anna copied Rupert and Abigail's behaviour, enjoying her first attempts at being a lady. The cakes were delicious. Raven poured his tea into his saucer to drink it. Anna squirmed in embarrassment but decided to say nothing. Rupert, ever the gentleman, ignored Raven's bad manners and carried on his conversation.

"So, you like horses Anna I assume," he said.

"Oh yes," said Anna, "very much. We have two Fell ponies. They are so gentle and kind. Raven and I ride them all the time."

"You must come and ride ours some time. We have a whole stable full. Lots of thoroughbreds and some hunters," Rupert said.

"Oh, that would be a dream," said Anna, "I've only ridden ponies before. I hear thoroughbreds are so fast. They gallop like the wind."

Rupert laughed.

"You'll love it Anna. Of course, Raven must try as well."

Raven grunted and carried on demolishing a piece of Victoria sponge.

"Do you ride Abigail?" asked Anna.

"Sometimes. I have a little grey pony that I ride on occasion. He is very patient with me. My legs don't work you see so I can't give commands with my feet. He listens to my voice though and I can still use the reins. I don't like to go too fast though."

Raven looked contemptuously at Abigail and declared, "Anna is the best rider in all the Dale. She is fearless. She's fantastic at everything she does in fact."

Rupert and Abigail smiled at him. It seemed nothing could put them out of temper. Their pale faces seemed incapable of showing deep passion.

In time, Anna and Raven expressed their sadness at having to leave and the housekeeper was called once more to lead them back to the car. Anna collapsed into the back seat of the Bentley in fits of giggles. Raven remained sullen.

"Oh Raven, wasn't that heavenly? I felt like I was walking on air the whole time. They live in such a refined world. It's so different from ours," said Anna.

"I prefer Dragon Fell," said Raven, "It's plain and simple. Like me. You know where you are with simple country folk. Not like them. Mealy mouthed, whey faced wimps."

"Raven, that's mean. You mustn't talk like that. I thought they were wonderful. So gentle and kind. And the house was just magical. Imagine living there."

Raven grimaced and scowled through the rest of the journey back to the farm. They got out of the car, thanked the bemused looking driver and hiked up the hill back to Dragon Fell. Anna couldn't stop talking about Odinsdale Hall to anyone who would listen. She started with Pearl and then moved on to Philip. When neither evinced much interest she retired to bed, her face beaming with delight at everything she had seen.

Anna took to going out riding every day in the hopes of seeing Rupert. After a week had gone by she wasn't disappointed. He was riding close to Dragon Fell on the moor and cantered up to Anna who was ambling along on her pony.

"Oh Rupert, I've missed you so much," said Anna.

"Me too. I was hoping to see you. That much is probably obvious. I have an idea.

Why don't we swap horses. This is Titan. He's strong but he won't misbehave with you. What about it?"

"Oh yes, I would love to ride him."

They swapped horses and Anna quickly grew comfortable with Titan. She galloped off over the moor with Rupert behind, striving to keep up on the old Fell pony. Anna soon pulled up, laughing with delight and waited for Rupert. They ambled along side by side, chatting gaily about all sorts of subjects. Rupert was an attentive listener and she enjoyed talking with him.

"Would you like to come back with me to see Dragon Fell?" said Anna.

"I would love to. Will Philip mind? Or Raven?"

"No. Of course not. They will both be out working. Pearl will be there. She keeps house for us. Dragon Fell is not grand like your house but it is my home. I do love it and I would like you to see it."

They turned and cantered back across the moor. Anna led them around the back of the farm to the stables, dismounted and put the pony into his stable. Titan was tied up outside. They went into the farmhouse via the backdoor.

"Pearl, Pearl! It's me. I've brought a visitor Rupert to see you."

Pearl appeared from doing the laundry looking shy and bashful. Rupert embraced her and kissed her cheek as was his habit with everyone. Pearl blushed in response.

"Please could you make us some tea Pearl? And maybe some of your lovely shortbread," said Anna.

Pearl bustled off and Anna and Rupert sat before the fire in the old armchairs. Rupert expressed his delight with everything, his manners never faltering. After they had finished their tea Anna gave him a tour of the house, showing him her favourite books and playthings. Then they went out and looked at the garden. The sun was shining but there was a nip in the wind, which was still blowing steadily, even in August. The roses were out, bravely fighting the breeze, the blooms nodding to each other. Bees were busy about their business and cabbage white butterflies fluttered around the pair. Rupert took Anna in his arms and kissed her full on the lips. Anna felt she was melting. Only Raven had ever kissed her like this before. She felt desire stir within her and returned the kiss with equal force. Anna realised she was in love with Rupert and Raven at the same time. She felt a strong pull to each of them but in completely different ways. She just wanted both but that was breaking the rules. What was she to do?

"You don't have electricity. That means no television. No radio. No wonder you are so well read and so deep," said Rupert.

"Well, I've never known any different. I was born here. I love to read but I would like to see a TV," said Anna.

"I must go," said Rupert, "they will be wondering what on earth happened to me. But you must come and visit again. And Raven. What about Sunday? I can show you the stables. And the TV. We can listen to music."

"Yes," said Anna, her eyes shining with joy.

Anna watched him ride away with a warm feeling in her heart.

That evening Anna was reading by the fire while Raven was cleaning his guns at her feet. They were so used to each other that words were not necessary. Their silence was companiable.

Anna broke it saying, "Rupert has invited us to the Hall again on Sunday."

"I'm not going," said Raven.

"Why ever not?"

"Because I don't like them. They're too posh for the likes of me. Everything's so la di da. We've nothing in common with them."

"Well, I like them. I'm going."

"Suit yourself."

***

As weeks and months passed Rupert and Anna were constant visitors to each other's homes. Sometimes Abigail came and sometimes she didn't. Desperate for friendship, Abigail showered Anna with gifts and compliments. She tried the same with Raven but found a stone wall in return. As the love between Rupert and Anna grew, Raven became more and more withdrawn. He spent all his time working on the farm or asleep. He spoke little and scowled often. Anna knew he was jealous of the time she spent with Rupert, but she could not bear to lose her new beau. She loved the attention she received at the Hall and the fine things she could live among. Rupert's parents adored her, and she loved Abigail as a dear friend. Her world had opened, and she was not going to let go.

***

One chilly November day Anna was waiting on the road at the bottom of the path to Dragon Fell waiting for the car to take her to Odinsdale Hall. She had been invited to Sunday lunch. Raven had refused to come. The wind was bitter and kept lifting Anna's coat. She slapped it down in irritation jumping up and down to keep warm. Her hair was under her woollen bunnet to stop it from blowing all around her face. The Bentley purred up to the gate and she opened the door and got in.

"Hi Robert, how are you?" she said to the chauffeur.

Robert turned round and smiled broadly at her.

"I'm doing great thanks. What a cold day. You'll be glad to get to the Hall," said Robert.

"Yes. I'm looking forward to it. We're having roast beef I believe. My favourite," said Anna.

In no time they arrived at the Hall and Robert steamed through the electric gates. He got out of the car to open the door for Anna and then drove the Bentley slowly back to the garage.

Anna rang the bell at the side of the old wooden door. Within a few minutes Mrs Harbottle appeared and welcomed Anna inside. Anna ran down the corridor and into the drawing room where the family were assembled. She rushed forward and kissed Rupert and threw her arms around him.

"I've missed you so much Rupes, I have had such a dull week without you," said Anna.

"Me too. I am delighted to see you," said Rupert.

Then Anna ran to Abigail to embrace her and then she did the same to Rupert's parents. Everyone smiled at Anna indulgently as she sat on the sofa next to Rupert. They held each other's hands gazing into each other's eyes. Shortly the dinner gong rang, and everyone filed into the dining room. Anna was seated opposite Rupert. He could not take his eyes off her for the duration of the lunch. The starter was prawn cocktail which Anna loved. She had learned not to wolf down her food but to take small teaspoons in a dainty manner.

"How is the farm going then Anna? You must miss the leadership of your father. Can Philip manage everything on his own?" said Rupert's father, Mr Fitzwilliam, smiling broadly at Anna.

"Yes. Philip works very hard, but he is doing well. He has Raven to help him of course. Everything is fine at Dragon Fell," said Anna, lying through her teeth to appear respectable.

"We are sad to not see Raven much these days," said Rupert's mother, Mrs Fitzwilliam.

"I'm afraid I can't persuade him to come. He's very busy with the farm," said Anna.

Rupert's mother was always dressed impeccably. She had a string of pearls around her neck, and she was wearing a pink cashmere sweater and black velvet slacks.

"I'm sure he would benefit from some polite society," she continued, "Look how much you have blossomed in our company. Abigail misses Raven."

"I'm sorry," said Anna, "I'll keep working on him."

The beef arrived and Rupert's father carved it up and gave everyone a slice. Anna loved Sunday lunch. There was so much food in the serving dishes and Anna helped herself to all types of food. There were huge Yorkshire puddings, roasted carrots and parsnips, cauliflower cheese, rich dark gravy and roast potatoes. Anna ate small bites of food daintily, but she finished all the food on her plate. Her appetite was hearty, but she didn't ever put on weight. Abigail, by contrast, ate little and picked at her food. She remained overly thin and sickly looking. For dessert, there was chocolate pudding. Anna found it utterly delicious. The Fitzwilliams were lucky enough to have a chef that cooked their meals. She had never tasted food prepared so well.

After lunch, Rupert wanted Anna all to himself. They went into the library on the pretext of wanting to find a book about racehorse breeding. Once in the library Rupert shut the door and settled himself next to Anna on the chaise longue. They began kissing and snuggling into each other. They were in Paradise together. Eventually they tired and Anna rested her head on Rupert's lap. He stroked her hair and told her about his latest point to point race. Eventually, the time came for Anna to leave, and Rupert walked her to the front door. The Bentley was already waiting to take her back to the farm. As Anna dozed in the back of the car a line of a song came into her head, "Loving both of them was breaking all the rules." Yes she did love Rupert and Raven at the same time, and she didn't know what to do about it.

***

Philip and Raven were now mortal enemies, but they endured each other with a quiet, simmering hatred. Raven was adult now, but he stayed because of Anna. He could not imagine his life without her. He knew Rupert was a threat. He needed a plan, but nothing presented itself. He did not earn enough money to whisk Anna away to another place. He started looking in the paper for farm hand positions. The pay was terrible, and he didn't think he would be able to keep Anna in luxury. How on earth did people get rich? Rupert had been born into it, but Raven had nothing. Lots of the jobs were live-in in a dormitory with other men. That would be no good for Anna. The rents in Odinsdale were too much for him. Lots of cottages had been turned into holiday lets. He dreamed of making it to Australia or the United States. In any case, he was not sure Anna would come away with him. Dragon Fell was all she had known.

One evening in late summer Philip returned from the local country show drunk as a lord. Anna and Raven had spent a pleasant day together walking in the fields. Their idyll was shattered by Philip singing and shouting as he stomped his way through the door and collapsed on the armchair. He glared at Anna across the room.

"You lazy bitch. What have you been doing all day? Pearl does everything and you do nowt. Think you're too good for us no with your new hoity toity friends?"

"No, I don't," said Anna calmly.

"Leave her alone!" shouted Raven.

"Make me," said Philip.

Raven bounded across the floor and took hold of Philip by his coat lapels.

"I said leave her alone," he hissed, his eyes blazing with anger.

Philip laughed in his face. Raven stepped back, moved his arm back quickly and punched Philip with full force right in the face. Philip staggered backwards and fell over, hitting his head hard on the stone flags beneath him. He blacked out and blood pooled around his head.

"He's dead, he's dead," screamed Pearl. She dropped to the floor, cradling his head in her arms.

"You don't know that Pearl. We must be calm. Don't touch him. I don't think he should be moved. Run to the road and flag down a car. Get it to take you to town for the doctor. Say it's an emergency. Go now Pearl," said Anna who felt strangely poised.

Raven stared down at Philip in horror as Pearl took a coat from the peg and ran down the path. Without a word he rushed upstairs, packed a small rucksack with a few items and the money from under his bed. He ran back downstairs and cradled Anna's face in his hands.

"I love you Anna. I will always love you. Until all the stars fall. Until there is nothing left. There will always be my love."

With that he exited through the door and ran down the path to the road.

Anna knew inside her heart that he had gone for good. He thought Philip was dead no doubt. Anna bent down to look at Philip. His face was ashen but when she listened to his chest she detected a heartbeat. He was still alive. Amid the horror and desolation of Raven leaving Anna felt hope that Philip would live. They had never been close but still, he was her brother and he had given her a home all these years. She fetched cloths from the kitchen drawer and mopped up the blood around his head. She sang and talked to him, saying his name, encouraging him to come back to her.

After what seemed like forever Anna heard the whirring of blades outside. She rushed out of the front door to see a rescue helicopter landing in the front garden. Anna had never seen such a thing before. Paramedics ran out with a stretcher and carried Philip away. Pearl appeared and hugged Anna tightly.
Philip lived.

Chapter Four

Life continued at Dragon Fell Farm. Philip came home from hospital and carried on working the land. He seemed much the same though he spoke a little slower and moved more carefully. Anna felt numb from Raven leaving. It was like a part of her own soul had been ripped out. Life was now a dream she was observing rather than living through. She spent most of her time in her bedroom reading, sleeping or just staring out of the window. The farm dogs kept her company, and she was grateful for their warm fur. The world seemed drained of colour. Most days she couldn't even be bothered to dress. She just stayed in her night dress with unbrushed hair. Anna had always thought that Raven would be part of her life, that he would never leave her. Yet he had. She had been scheming to marry Rupert but keep Raven close. Her hopes were ash. She had lost interest in all the things she previously loved. She no longer went riding or walking on the moor. Letters from Rupert went unanswered. Pearl brought up her meals, but she ate little. Anna slept with the window open so that she could feel the wind from the Dale on her face. Pearl came in once she had fallen asleep and closed it.

One morning there was a bang at the door. Pearl ran up to Anna's room to tell her that Rupert had come calling. Anna looked listlessly up from her bed. She had not bothered to dress and her hair hung lank around her shoulders.

"What should I say to him?" said Pearl.

"Tell him to go away. I have no desire to see anyone," said Anna.

As Pearl turned to go Rupert appeared behind her in the doorway. He rushed to Anna's bedside and held her close.

"Oh Anna, Anna. What has happened to you? I heard about Raven leaving. The servants love to gossip. I'm so sorry. But you look so ill. You must get well. Life goes on. I want to help you," said Rupert.

Anna smiled weakly at him. They spent the day together. Rupert read to her and told her stories. He bragged about his big dreams for the future.

"You know Anna. I am going to be the greatest racehorse owner in all of Yorkshire. A horse of mine will win the Grand National, you'll see. Even the Queen will be jealous of my success. And Odinsdale Hall will be used. We could remake some of the outbuildings as holiday lets. I will let out the main hall for functions: wedding banquets and such. Then maybe shooting parties: deerstalking and grouse. There are foreigners will pay a fortune for such opportunities. I shall be the richest man for miles around."

"That sounds wonderful," said Anna, "but I'm just happy living a quiet life in the Dale. I love the moor, nature and my books."

"Well, nobody is stopping you doing all that," said Rupert, smiling at her simplicity that he loved so much.

Over the weeks that followed Anna rallied. Her body was too strong to wither and die. Her mind almost recovered from the loss though she smiled less and there was a deep sadness that rested in her eyes. Rupert indulged her and she enjoyed his company. They went riding and walking together and she spent much time at Odinsdale Hall. Anna learned to be a lady by copying the manners and behaviour of Abigail. Even her accent softened as she lengthened her vowels in the presence of her new friends.

***

One Thursday evening, Anna, Rupert and Abigail were watching Top of the Pops on the little television in the corner of the sitting room. This programme had become a firm favourite of Anna's.

"I love Top of the Pops," said Anna, "the bands seem so glamorous, and the women are beautiful and most of the men so handsome. It's so exciting seeing what is at the top of the charts each week. Isn't it amazing that we can watch what is happening in London on a little box? It's like magic. This programme is my favourite. And I like Little House on the Prairie as well. Maybe because it's a bit like Dragon Fell Farm."

"One day we will go to London, and I will show it all for real. We will have tea at the Ritz and then walk around Hyde Park."

Rupert had his arm around Anna, and they were cosily ensconced, giggling, chatting and eating crisps. After the programme had ended Rupert rode with Anna back to Dragon Fell. It was summer now and the evenings were light. They enjoyed looking at the blooming heather as they rode by. The sun was just setting on the hill with a wondrous orange glow. As they walked to the entrance to the stables Rupert turned his horse close to Anna.

"I've been thinking. We get on so well you and me. You are lonely here and I am lonely at Odinsdale. What about if we got married? We could all live together at the Hall. You and Abigail are such great friends. It would be perfect. Would you like that? Should I ask Philip? Do you think that's the proper thing?"

Anna was not surprised. It seemed like the natural course of events.

"Yes," she said simply, dismounted and rode into the stables.

Anna went into the house and curled up in the armchair. Philip came and sat opposite her looking very pleased with himself.

"I have news, Anna," he said. "I've ordered what they call a mail order bride. From Thailand. We have been writing to each other for months. She wants to marry me. She is coming on the train tomorrow. I'm meeting her at the station. I've arranged a small ceremony in the church with the vicar. Just a couple of witnesses needed. Would you like to be a witness?"

Anna looked up at Philip startled.

"Have you thought this through Philip? It seems a bit sudden. You haven't even met. What if you don't get on?" said Anna.

"We do get on. We've been writing for ages. She's seen my photo and I've seen hers. She's beautiful. We'll be fine."

"Well, it's your life. I have news of my own. Rupert is going to ask you if he can marry me."

"Splendid, splendid. So, everything will work out. That's a fantastic idea. You and Rupert get on so well."

Kanshi arrived the next day. She was small and thin and kept her eyes lowered when she first came into the kitchen. Anna put out her hand and was surprised to see Kanshi bow and put her hands together like a prayer. Not sure what to do, Anna repeated the same actions back to Kanshi. Gaining confidence, Kanshi looked about the kitchen, admiring the copper pans hanging up, the blackness of the range and the smooth stone flags on the floor.

"It's all so clean and beautiful," she said, "Everything lovely."

"I'm glad you like it. I'm afraid we are a bit behind the times here. There is no running water or electricity. Pearl works so hard to keep everything nice. We are isolated. I think most people in the Dale think we're a bit odd but it's all I've ever known."

"I like it very much," said Kanshi, smiling broadly now.

"Come on. I'll show you the rest of the farm," said Philip, his eyes shining with happiness. They both disappeared outside for hours. Pearl made up a makeshift bed for Kanshi in the kitchen as there were no spare bedrooms and it didn't seem proper for her to go in with Philip before marriage.

The next morning was the wedding day. Philip donned his best suit. He had ordered a wedding dress for Kanshi. Anna and Pearl helped her dress with excited giggles. It was a long white shift of beautiful lace. Kanshi looked breathtaking. The service in the local village church was simple with a bemused looking vicar, the bride and groom, Anna,

Pearl and two parishioner volunteers who were dragooned into attending as witnesses. Kanshi looked delighted. Back at the farm Pearl had prepared a feast of roast lamb with all the trimmings and a trifle for afterwards. Anna hoped the couple would be happy together. Philip and Kanshi retired to Philip's room early leaving Anna and Pearl to wash up the dishes. They heard banging and sighs from the bedroom, then sounds like an animal in pain. Pearl and Anna giggled together. Anna had seen animals on the farm mate with each other enough times to know something about sex, but the human version was still a mystery to her.

The following morning Rupert appeared at Dragon Fell to ask for Anna's hand in marriage. Philip broke out the home-made fruit wine and by midday they were both pleasantly drunk, reminiscing about their childhoods and clapping each other on the back like old pals.

"The thing about women see is you've got to show them who's boss. Like me and Kanshi. She's a lovely old-fashioned girl, quiet and gentle. Now Anna, she's a different kettle of fish altogether. Needs a firm hand. Spirited, that's what," said Philip.

"But I like that about her. She is so strong and the best rider in the Dale. A bit of spirit is a good thing in a girl," said Rupert.

"Happen, happen," said Philip, pouring himself another wine.

Anna, upstairs, listening at the door could hear every word. She hugged herself with delight. Married to Rupert, she would be the grandest lady in the district. She would love to see their faces in the village when she drove in with the Bentley.

"So, Philip. May I have your sister's hand in marriage?" said Rupert, concentrating on not dropping his glass as his vision blurred.

"I do solemnly declare that you may," said Philip pompously.

They chinked their glasses together and collapsed into fits of laughter.

So that was that. The great wedding day approached. Rupert's parents poured money into the occasion. It was the society wedding of the year in the quiet Dale. Hundreds of guests were invited. There were the great and the good of Odinsdale, people from the horseracing community, old university friends of Mr Fitzwilliam, and elderly relatives from all corners of the Kingdom. The main protagonists wore tailcoats and top hats. Anna arrived in a horse drawn carriage with black horses pulling it with white feathers in their headbands. Her dress came from a designer in London, and it had a huge, long train that Anna tripped over as she left the carriage. Pearl and Abigail were bridesmaids in matching blue silk dresses. Afterwards there was a banquet at the Hall. There were all kinds of roast meats and an ice swan as a centrepiece. Anna was too breathless to eat very much. It was a perfect dream but somehow she could not enjoy it. Rupert, sitting beside her, gazed at her adoringly.

"Are you happy, Anna?" he said.

"Completely," Anna lied.

"We are going to have the most perfect life together, you'll see," Rupert said.

Anna took a sip of wine and surveyed all the dull people, almost none of whom she knew. It hit her like a brick that she had made the wrong decision. She could have married Raven and kept Rupert as a friend. Her mind kept thinking of her childhood companion. It should have been him. All the refinement and fripperies meant little to her. She would have been happy with Raven in a little cottage on the moor, with the birds of prey for company. Yet here she was, a fine lady. She wondered where on earth Raven was. She often heard him calling to her in dreams, wandering the moor like they had as children. Their bond had grown over years until they seemed part of each other. Raven was a wolf and Rupert a helpless lamb. Of course, life with Rupert was easy but Anna had grown up at Dragon Fell, as hard as the stone on the moor. She and Rupert were not the same, almost as if they were different species.

Anna went to live at Odinsdale Hall, settling into a calm, domestic life with Rupert, Abigail and their increasingly infirm parents. She lost touch with Dragon Fell, not hearing what was going on with Philip and Kanshi. She missed Pearl like an ache. Pearl had been like a sister to her. Rupert was the perfect, doting husband and Anna spent her days in idleness. She had a fine grey thoroughbred to ride on the moor now who could gallop faster than wind. She had a whole library of books to read and the television and radio to divert her. Abigail was fun to talk to and they spent many hours scouring magazines, chatting about TV shows and playing with the assortment of dogs. Everything appeared perfect. Anna knew she should have been happy, but she could not settle without Raven. Her life felt silly and frivolous. There was no purpose. As time went on, Anna suffered from morose moods. She spent whole days in bed, just staring at the ceiling. Then she would recover and be back to herself, laughing as she ran through the corridors, pushing Abigail's chair, whooping like a wild animal. Why could Anna not be truly happy? She did not know the answer, but she felt that her and Raven had a destiny together that had been broken.

Anna often walked in the grounds of Odinsdale Hall. Everything was easier here. Even in winter, the weather was milder than Dragon Fell and the snow didn't stay on the ground so long. In the summer, the gardens were full of roses and insects buzzed around making the whole place feel alive. Anna made a pet of a robin and fed it from her hand. Yet Anna missed the harshness of Dragon Fell Farm. It was part of her soul. She felt like she was living someone else's life, observing, not living within it.

The time came that Rupert's parents died. They were content to go as they had lived, full happy lives. They had been glad to see Rupert married but worried about Abigail. They were buried in the village churchyard and had two elaborate gravestones with angels blowing trumpets adorning them. Rupert inherited Odinsdale Hall in the will but

Abigail was well provided for. She inherited a portfolio of stocks and shares and she had more than enough to live on for the rest of her life.

Chapter Five

Winter came again to Dragon Fell Farm. Snow blanketed the ground thickly. The wind whistled down the chimneys and cold drafts stalked the hallways and crept under the doors. Water had turned to ice in the pails in the kitchen. Kanshi was eight months pregnant. She was curled by the fire in 'the house'. Kanshi had a bed made up permanently by the fire so she could stay warm. She stoked the fire through the night with coal. She found the winter so hard, but she didn't complain. Her dreams were full of the warmth and vibrancy of Thailand, but she was grateful for Philip and the food she had to eat. She felt protected and safe. It was early afternoon, but it already felt dark. Kanshi was overjoyed at the baby growing inside her. She sang to it softly as she watched the flames dance. Pearl was banging around in the kitchen, cleaning up. Suddenly, Kanshi felt pain in her abdomen like she had never felt before.

"Pearl, Pearl," Kanshi shouted.

Pearl came running and could see immediately what was wrong as Kanshi was doubled over in pain. The baby was coming too early. Pearl guided Kanshi to lie down on the makeshift bed. She ran into the fields to find Philip. As she shouted his name her words were lost in the wind. She ran around but couldn't find him. He must have gone up on the moor to find a lost sheep. Pearl ran back into the house.

Kanshi was lying on the makeshift bed moaning in pain. She called for Philip in between breaths.

"I can't find him," said Pearl.

Pearl didn't know what to do. She was torn between staying with Kanshi or running down the road for the doctor. But she couldn't leave Kanshi on her own. If only Philip was here. Pearl would have to manage herself. She undressed Kanshi's lower half and made a tent out of the bedsheet. She put Kanshi's legs in what she assumed to be the appropriate position. Instinct was taking over as Pearl knew nothing about childbirth.

"Kanshi, see if you can push. Push the baby out," said Pearl.

Kanshi screamed as if she had been burned with a thousand red hot pokers. She pushed and Pearl could just see something. Instead of a head it was a foot. The baby was breached. Pearl tried to pull the foot, but it didn't budge. Blood was starting to spurt out.

"Push Kanshi push," Pearl screamed.

The next few hours passed in a blur to Pearl. She tried all different tactics. She pulled, she pushed, she twisted what she could feel of the baby. All the while Kanshi was screaming in agony. Somehow Pearl managed to get the baby out. It laid on the floor of the farm, his face screwed up in rage. Yes it was a boy. Pearl cut the umbilical cord with the kitchen knife and wrapped the baby up in a blanket. She placed him on the kitchen table and returned to Kanshi. Blood was pooling all around her, dripping on the stone flags. Pearl fetched a damp cloth and bathed the mother's sweating face. Kanshi was no longer fully aware. She was murmuring something Pearl could not understand and her eyes were closed. Pearl kept talking to her, begging her to stay awake, and telling her what a fine son she had. Kanshi began slipping away. Pearl could see the life draining out of her and her skin became colder and colder to the touch. Pearl listened for a heartbeat and found none. Kanshi had gone. Pearl's face was horror struck but she returned to the baby. He was crying pitifully. Pearl went to the pantry and found some cow's milk. She placed it in a baby bottle which Kanshi had bought and warmed the milk by the fire. She didn't know if her actions were right or not, but the baby needed milk and Pearl had none. She cradled the child in her arms by the fire and fed him from the bottle. The warm milk calmed him, and he fed contentedly. After the bottle was empty Pearl rocked him gently and he drifted off to sleep. Hours seemed to pass, and Pearl fell asleep herself. She was awakened by Philip shouting in her face.

"Pearl, Pearl! What the hell has happened? What have you done you stupid cow?"

Pearl started to cry. In between sobs she explained about the breach birth and that Kanshi had died.

Philip, white with fury, took the baby from Pearl. As he gazed at the child his face seemed to soften temporarily. Then he turned to the servant girl with real hatred in his face.

"Run for the doctor," he snarled at Pearl.

Pearl ran from the house with terror in her heart. She felt like she had killed Kanshi. The look of hatred on Philip's face had shocked her to the core. Pearl did not go for the doctor. She ran the two miles home to her mother like the devil himself was chasing her. She never returned to Dragon Fell Farm. In time, Anna heard what had happened and sent for her to be a helper at Odinsdale Hall. Pearl settled in well with her beloved Anna and found she had much less to do than she had at the farm. She was now a lady's maid to Anna. She had a lovely room of her own at the back of the house with a comfortable bed and pretty flower pattern wallpaper. She even had her own portable TV so that she could watch shows in the evening.

That was the night that peace seemed to depart from Dragon Fell Farm. The red dragon had not protected Kanshi. She had not been born there and worshipped other gods. The dragon had allowed her to die like Anna's mother had before her.

Kanshi was buried in the village churchyard in a private ceremony. It was just Philip, the baby and the vicar. It was still snowing on the day of the funeral. The coffin had to be carried down the fields to the road by hand. Philip hired some local labourers to help him. Then she was loaded on to the hearse and taken to the church. The vicar droned on in his interminable way. Philip no longer believed in the promise of Heaven or indeed in anything. Eventually, the coffin was carried out into the church yard and Kanshi was lowered into the Earth. Philip threw a clod of soil on to the coffin and turned away. The snow fell heavier and heavier, deadening sound. His sadness was too deep for tears. From that day Philip was morose. He walked all the way back from the miserable lonely funeral with his son in his arms. He named the child James. He made enquiries in the village for a nanny cum housekeeper and found no takers. The locals said the farm was cursed. He advertised in the paper and a shy girl from Leeds arrived one day with a small rucksack and the clothes she stood up in. This was Molly. She was desperate enough to take the job with the angry man that Philip had become. She looked after James well and kept him out of Philip's way when dark moods overcame him.

Philip fell into darkness. He spent his days in The Red Lion in the village and wended his way home in the evenings drunk and dishevelled. He fell into his dinner most evenings and slept where he sat. Molly tiptoed around him clearing up his mess and took James with her to sleep in the little attic room that has been Pearl's. Philip lost interest in the farm and hired a young man from the village to run things for him. Ben came in a little car that he parked on the main road and then walked through the fields to the farm. In the evening he walked back to his car and went home to his parents' house in the village. Ben learned the work of the farm fast. He tended the sheep and cattle and kept out of Philip's way. He enjoyed working with the animals and was only seen in the house at noon for his dinner that Molly prepared.

Life went on. One evening, Philip invited men from the village back to the farm after the pub had closed. They continued drinking and playing cards. They were playing for money. Molly lay in bed with James listening to the racket as they shouted and swore as they slapped the cards down. They were drinking whiskey. When Molly woke the next day and crept downstairs they were still sleeping where they had sat. The dining table was strewn with empty bottles, glasses and cigarette papers. Molly made some porridge for James and disappeared back upstairs with it. She didn't want to sit with such people. As she fed James and looked at his innocent little face she feared for him. She had nowhere to go, and he needed her. She couldn't leave him with Philip. She would have to stay whatever happened. As the morning wore on the visitors eventually left. Molly went downstairs and let James play on the floor while she tidied up the mess they had left behind. Philip went out again in the clothes he had been wearing all night. Hours later he returned looking furtive and arranged little packets on the table. In each he poured something into each one that looked like herbs. In others he placed pills and white powder. Molly knew it was drugs. She said nothing and retreated upstairs with James. She cried to herself as she rocked James in her arms. Things went from bad to worse.

Philip sold drugs from the house. All kinds of strange people turned up at all times of the day and night. Some stayed for days and even weeks. Philip let some of them camp in the fields. They set up tents and played guitars and danced around. A few made benders out of tarpaulins and tree branches. They lit fires and brewed tea. Several scrawny dogs appeared. Generators meant they had electricity. They blared music from morning until night. Some appeared blind drunk by 10 am. They had long hair and brightly coloured clothes and never washed. Molly tried her best to keep the house tidy and she kept James away from the guests as best she could. They went walking together across the moors and in the evenings she read to him in her room by candlelight. In the winter, many of the guests melted away, but Philip continued with his drug selling and late-night drinking parties.

One spring day Molly was walking through the garden with James by her side. There was a canvas tent just beside the front door. As Molly passed by a long-haired man came out with some strange pipe arrangement in his hands. He passed the pipe to Molly, but she refused to take it. He was wearing a waistcoat over a bare chest, and he also had wide trousers covering his lower half. She could see black hairs covering his chest. His eyes were red with inflammation.

"Come on, it will do you good. It's only woodbine, not dope. It will calm you."

"I don't need to be calm thank you," said Molly stiffly, "I am perfectly calm already."

The strange man laughed and went back inside his tent. As Molly continued, two girls were dancing with each other, laughing incessantly and making wide movements with their arms. They stared at Molly as if she was some strange creature before adjusting the flowers in each other's long, flowing hair.

Molly sighed with irritation. It was nigh on impossible to look after James in such an environment, but she tried her best. She kept him outside with her as long as she could when the weather was fine. They walked for miles across the moor. Today she loaded him up on the old Fell pony so that his legs wouldn't get so tired. As she was ambling along leading the pony along a sheep track she spied a rider in the distance. It was a fine lady riding side saddle on a black thoroughbred. She had a bowler hat on and a riding habit with a wide skirt for the side saddle. The lady cantered closer to Molly and then slowed to a walk as she came nearer. It was Anna. She was practising side saddle for the ladies' class at The Yorkshire Show.

"Hello, I don't think I've seen you in these parts before," said Anna.

"I'm Molly. I work at Dragon Fell Farm. This is James, Philip's son."

"Oh my God," said Molly, "Philip is my brother. So, James is my nephew. Hello James."

James smiled up at Anna but didn't say anything.

"So how are things there?" said Anna.

"Well not good. I, I..." Molly began and then burst into tears.

"There, there. Don't take on so. What on earth is the matter?"

So, Molly, who had had nobody to talk to for many months, told Anna the whole story. She told about the drunkenness, the drug selling, the strange people camping in the garden, the endless parade of ne'er do wells in the house and the difficulty of keeping James away from the bawdiness and the foul language. Anna listened in horror. She wanted to take James away with her there and then, but he was Philip's son, and the action probably wasn't legal.

"I don't know what to do," Anna wailed.

"I don't know if there is anything we can do. I wouldn't like James to be taken away, but things seem to be going from bad to worse. I am just trying to keep him safe," said Molly.

"I'm riding back with you. Hop up beside me. I need to see for myself."

Anna scrambled up on to the big thoroughbred with the help of a nearby stone keeping tight hold of the lead rein with James and the fell pony at the end of it. They walked back to Dragon Fell in quiet procession.

Anna took the horses round to the back and tied them up. Then she marched to the front door and banged on it. The door was opened by somebody she did not recognise. He was a strange looking fellow. His eyes were shrunken in his head, and he looked like he had not eaten for weeks. His cheekbones jutted out from his face.

"I'm Anna from Odinsdale Hall. Let me through," said Anna.

The man wordlessly opened the door wider and let Anna into the house. Inside was a shocking scene. Philip was asleep by the fire with half a bottle of whisky in his hand. A couple were copulating on the floor like dogs. The farm table was strewn with cigarette packets, powders and pills. An assortment of men was lounging around in various states of stupor. One look was enough. She did not wake Philip but scribbled a note on some paper she had in her habit pocket. She wrote that she had taken James and if he wanted to do anything about it she would contact social services and the police. If he wanted to keep his freedom he would let James alone. She tucked the paper into Philip's lap.

Anna swept out and returned to the yard where Molly and James were waiting. Fearing that Philip would wake up she hoisted James in front of her saddle and leaped up behind him.

"Molly, I'm taking James to Odinsdale Hall. You can follow on with the pony. Can you ride?"

"I'm afraid not. I never learned. I could just lead him though," said Molly.

"Good girl. Just keep going down the hill until you get to the Hall. You can't go wrong," said Anna.

Then she galloped off in a haze of dust to the Hall. Molly, in shock, ambled down the path at a snail's pace with the elderly pony, wondering what was to become of her. One thing was certain, she didn't want to go back to Leeds.

So it came to pass that both Molly and James stayed at Odinsdale Hall with Anna and Rupert. Philip did not come to call. Anna heard nothing from him. No police nor social workers visited much to Anna's relief. She avoided Dragon Fell Farm on her rides and walks. James was kept safe in the grounds of the Hall. Rupert feared James would be snatched by Philip, so he kept him secluded. Molly was employed as James's nanny. Everyone was safe together at Odinsdale Hall.

***

Three years passed in such a fashion. Under Molly's care James grew big and strong. Anna and Abigail also played with him in the nursery. He was showered with toys and generally spoiled rotten. He had a sweet nature though and loved his new family. Days were spent playing and walking in the grounds. James was often to be seen in his toy car, tooting at the gardeners. He would run in the house with posies of flowers for Molly and Pearl.

One morning, Anna was admiring herself in a new dress she had just ordered. It was blue silk. As she surveyed her figure she noticed she was considerably fatter. She popped on to the scales and realised she was several pounds heavier than usual. She did not keep track of her periods but had the sense she hadn't had one for a while. Realisation dawned she might be pregnant. Anna changed into a tweed suit and ordered the car to take her into the local market town. She asked the chauffeur to wait and went to the chemist. She bought a pregnancy test and several other items she didn't need so that she was not embarrassed. Then, feeling famished, she bought some little cakes from the bakers and returned to the car. Once back at the Hall she rushed up to her bedroom to take the test. Yes. It was positive. Anna was pregnant.

No home birth for Anna. At the appointed time she was driven to the hospital in Durham. Rupert was away at a horse sale in Ireland so wasn't there for the birth. She felt surreal during the journey as if it was all happening to someone else. On arrival, a haughty nurse showed her into a private room, and she undressed and got into bed. Everything smelled strangely of something chemical like disinfectant. Somebody had thoughtfully arranged some roses in a vase on the windowsill. The contractions were coming closer together now and she was in considerable pain. Bossy midwives appeared and told her how to breathe. Without much fuss or time baby Louisa slipped into the world. Anna felt a surge of elation when the birth was over. Louisa was tidied up by the nurses and presented to her. Anna felt a bond of love for the child. She knew the baby would make Rupert happy.

Chapter Six

Anna recovered from her pregnancy at Odinsdale Hall, amusing herself in the house and grounds. She spent time with Pearl during the day when Rupert was out and about managing the estate. Anna was not a natural mother and let Pearl look after the baby most of the time. Molly and Pearl became friends, and they had fun together with James and Louisa. The children played together in the huge nursery. They were showered with toys from Rupert. They were both given Shetland ponies to learn to ride called Nosferatu and Bram by Anna as some kind of joke.

***

The best Christmas was when Louisa was three and James was six. The day before Christmas Eve the whole family went on a trip to Durham. Snow was carpeting the ground making the whole city look magical. Louisa and James had warm coats, so they didn't mind the cold. Anna was wearing a sable fur coat that had belonged to old Mrs Fitzwilliam. Pearl and Molly had woollen coats with warm mittens and bobble hats. Pearl was pushing Abigail in her wheelchair. Abigail looked like a fairy tale in a white fur wrap and matching fur hat. Rupert was also resplendent in a tweed suit and navy overcoat. They meandered around the narrow streets of the city, visiting all the shops. The toy shop was a favourite and the children were allowed to pick a special present each. Louisa chose a doll that looked remarkably like a real baby and James picked out a toy train. Pleased with themselves they all trooped along to a little café and had hot chocolate and cakes. The little place was packed with Christmas revellers all in a merry Christmas mood. They ventured outside and joined in with some carollers belting out Christmas favourites for all they were worth. Then they gazed at the tableau outside the cathedral where children were dressed as angels, Joseph and the Virgin Mary with a little doll in a crib as Jesus. Feeling full of good cheer, they all went back to the car to be driven back to Odinsdale Hall. Molly hugged herself with delight that she had found such a good position with such a wonderfully kind family. She was so happy that James was growing up in such a beneficial environment.

Christmas Eve passed interminably for the children who couldn't wait for Santa. They rushed up and down the nursery excitedly and argued over toys, squabbling with the stress of anticipation. Molly, worn to a frazzle with trying to manage the children's excitement put them to bed early with a cup of warm milk each. While they were drinking up she read them Christmas poems and sang them carols. Eventually, they fell asleep smiling.

On Christmas morning, James woke first at six. He ran into Louisa's room and hauled her out of bed. They ran down the stairs to the drawing room where the Christmas tree was. It was a huge fir that had been cut from their own estate, decorated with lights and baubles of all colours. Underneath was a pile of presents in red and blue wrappers. The children squealed in delight and set about ripping open the presents. There were toys, games, chocolates and even new bicycles for each of them. The adults came in soon after and smiled indulgently as they showed off their new things, babbling in excitement. The children watched some children's television for the rest of the morning, sitting next to each other on the Persian rug cross legged, smiling and laughing with each other.

Christmas lunch was a grand affair. They had turkey with all the trimmings and Christmas pudding for dessert. The table was dressed with Christmas ornaments and candles. The best china was used. It was so beautiful with little roses painted on it. There was much jollity as James told several bad jokes, but everyone laughed anyway. After lunch, they watched the Queen's speech on the television and then enjoyed a game of charades. The children went to bed that night feeling like the happiest children in England. All were happy at Odinsdale Hall except Anna. Of course, she pretended to be happy. She joined in with everything, laughing and smiling but inside she felt a deadening.

Anna spent most of her good days walking and riding. She loved being out on the moor among the animals and the birds. She spent much time alone as Rupert was so busy with all his businesses. In her lighter moods she would spend time with the children but their exuberance tired her quickly and she would make an excuse to leave. Sometimes, she would push Abigail around the grounds, chatting about the latest TV shows and articles she had read in magazines. She spent evenings with Rupert, watching TV or reading. Sometimes they listened to classical music together. Rupert was the perfect husband. They made love once a week and Anna had a generous allowance to spend on clothes and trinkets.

Sadness came in waves. On her worst days she just about managed to bathe and dress herself before collapsing in the library with a "Do not disturb" sign on the door. She would read, or pretend to read, often just staring into space, remembering childhood days and wondering about Raven. She swore he came to her in dreams, hugging her and touching her cheek, telling her everything would be all right.

One dreary winter afternoon Anna was reading in the library alone, lazing on the chaise long feeling blue and weary. Such moods had become more common with her recently. As she lay there she could hear rain starting, tapping at the window and thunder crashed in the distance. A knock at the door roused her from her semi-slumber and she said, "Come."

The housekeeper appeared looked slightly agitated.

"There is a gentleman at the door asking to see you, Madam," said the woman.

"A gentleman. Asking for me?" said Anna incredulously, "Who on earth could it be? I don't know anyone."

"He says his name is Raven," said the housekeeper.

"Oh, my God. Raven! Raven! Let him up at once."

Anna leaped up and began tidying her hair and pinching her cheeks to try to bring some colour into them.

After a few moments Raven was there in the doorway. He moved into the room and stood in front of the window. As if on cue, a lightning bolt illuminated him as he stood there. Anna gasped at his transformation. Hardly any of the old Raven was in evidence now. Gone was the slouching, scowling, dirty farm boy of old. Instead, there was a tall, slender man with perfectly groomed dark hair. He was dressed for the country with a well-fitting Tweed suit with a waistcoat underneath. He had a smooth, wooden walking stick in his hand with a brass handle. He gazed at Anna with a sense of wonder on his face as if he could not believe she was real. To Raven, it seemed as if everything in the world had faded away and there was just Anna standing there.

Within a minute they leaped towards each other and embraced fiercely. Raven kissed Anna full on the mouth repeatedly. It was as if time froze, and they were locked together forever.

Their joy was shattered by the door opening and Rupert standing there aghast.

"What the devil is going on here?" he said.

Anna and Raven sprang apart.

Anna said, "Look Rupert. It's Raven. He's returned. Isn't it wonderful?"

"Wonderful? The fiend is kissing my wife behind my back. How dare you?" said Rupert.

Raven spoke with perfect composure, "If you would forgive me Rupert. We were just overwhelmed as old friends who have not seen each other for so long."

"No, I won't forgive you, get out of my house and don't ever come back. I forbid you to see Anna or anyone else in my household."

Raven walked calmy to the door and exited the house. Rupert was red in the face and visibly shaking. Anna scowled at her husband.

"Rupert, you evil man. How could you ban Raven? He's a part of me, part of my soul, my heart."

With that she collapsed in a faint on the floor. Rupert left the room and asked Pearl to put her to bed. Pearl and Molly carried Anna up to her room, undressed her and put on her nightdress. All the while, she was muttering and mumbling as if having a nightmare. She seemed to be somewhere between two worlds. The shock of seeing Raven again and then losing him so quickly seemed to have affected her mind. Pearl stayed by Anna's side as she tossed and turned and moaned. She was burning up to the touch and sometimes foamed at the mouth. Pearl tried to persuade her to drink water which she refused. She bathed her face and spoke soothingly but nothing she did seemed to make any difference. Pearl despatched Molly to tell Rupert. He did not look in on Anna but told Molly to telephone the doctor to come for a visit. Then he went out riding.

Dr Tate arrived. He was a kindly, slightly overweight man dressed in a Tweed jacket and faded brown corduroys. He examined Anna as she slept and then diagnosed anxiety and conversion disorder. He prescribed pills and bedrest and went away again. Anna was suffering from stress and Dr Tate suggested she may have histrionic personality disorder. Pearl worried that Anna would be sent away. She tried her best to care for Anna to avoid this outcome. She spent day and night sitting in a chair next to the bed. She fed Anna when she could and provided plenty of fluids in the form of tea and herbal concoctions. Rupert did not come near. Pearl read to Anna, anything and everything, magazines, the newspaper, old books. She left the TV on when she had to leave the room, so Anna didn't feel alone. Two border terriers were despatched to Anna's bedroom to provide furry comfort. Anna had hours of lucidity when it seemed she was quite normal again and then she would sink into a semi-coma, seeming unaware of her surroundings.

The day he was banished from Odinsdale Hall Raven walked up the hill to Dragon Fell Farm. On arrival he knocked at the door but received no answer. He pushed it and walked in. If he was shocked by the disarray all around him he didn't show it in his face. Philip was dozing by the fire with several old dogs at his feet.

"Good evening to you sir," said Raven.

Philip peered up from his stupor.

"It's you. It's you. The devil himself. You tried to kill me," said Philip.

"But here you are, very much alive," said Raven.

"I am indeed. But you see I have fallen far since those days. My wife died. The devil has taken me to drink and gambling as you see."

"I would very much like to stay here. I have a fondness for the old place. I'll pay you handsomely for bed and board. What do you say?" said Raven.

Philip's eyes gleamed at the thought of money, and he acquiesced to Raven's request.

So it was that Raven took up residence once more at Dragon Fell Farm. He moved into Anna's old room and made it his own. He had money to burn. Nobody knew where it had come from, and Raven didn't tell. He had new furniture sent up to the farm and made the bedroom pleasant. There was a brass bedstead and a wooden writing desk. He had several items of Chinoiserie including a screen painted with beautiful scenes of nature and a large chest. Raven spent his days writing and walking on the moor. In the evenings, he joined in the carousing downstairs. He pretended to drink but hardly a drop passed his lips. He was an expert card player and began to systematically drain Philip of what money he had retained. Raven was fastidious now that he was a grown man and gone were the slovenly ways of his childhood. He employed a young man called John from the village to clean and tidy the house. Dragon Fell was no place for a girl now. Parcels of food were sent for from various local establishments to the box at the field gate. John was sent daily to retrieve them, and he learned to cook reasonably well for Raven. Many weeks passed in such a fashion.

Philip deteriorated under the careful manipulation of Raven. He was mostly drunk from morning until night and Raven kept a plentiful supply of spirits to tempt him. The alcohol addled his brain so that his judgement at card games was severely impaired. Raven kept a careful tally of his losses, noting everything down in an accounts book. In time Philip had nothing left to bet with so he borrowed money from Raven to keep playing. One Saturday evening Philip had roused himself enough to walk to the pub in the village. It was raining heavily all the way there, but Philip kept going. He needed a change from the farm. Once there he ensconced himself in the inglenook fireplace with a cigarette and a glass of brandy. Some of the locals started singing an old folk song about a soldier and Prince Albert and fighting for your country. Philip joined in smiling to himself. He started to cry quietly as he thought back to childhood and those carefree days with Anna and Raven. He thought of Kanshi and how he ached for her. He could not stop the pain in his heart however much he drank. He thought about what a mess he had made of it all. If only he had behaved better. If only Kanshi could have lived. He thought of James, the child he had given away. While musing in this way he seemed to see Kanshi hovering in front of him, just a few feet away. It couldn't be and yet there she was. Philip stood up to try to be close to her and in that moment his heart stopped beating and he fell to the floor. So was the sad end of Philip who was buried in the churchyard next to Kanshi.

Raven inherited the farm lock, stock and barrel. It was all in order. He had won the place in a game of cards and Philip owed him thousands of pounds on top of that. The solicitor could do nothing but award the farm to Raven. He had won his heart's desire at last. Raven banished the drunks and the hippies from the farm and set about a program of renovation. Workmen and decorators came to fix up the place, painting, hammering and making good. Dragon Fell was now fit for a country gentleman. Raven even paid the electricity company a huge amount to join the farm to the national grid. Plumbing was also installed to make a modern bathroom. Electric radiators were placed in every room and even several telephones. Raven paid for a private road to be laid from the main thoroughfare below the farm. He fixed a gate on the entrance to the byway and erected a large sign with Dragon Fell Farm written on in gold lettering. Dragon Fell had arrived at the modern world. Raven now surmised it was a place fit for Anna. He schemed to get her back. He would do it if it killed him. Raven knew nothing of Anna's illness. He assumed she was still in wedded bliss. He continued his walks on the hills and managing his business affairs. In the evening he read books that he had delivered from the local bookshop. He had no interest in television and didn't bother getting one.

The dragon withdrew his protective breath from Dragon Fell Farm. He was angered by the electricity pylons' crackle and the noise of the road. He disappeared into the other world, deep inside the Earth.

One gloomy day Raven was walking and ruminating in his usual way across the moor. He walked down almost to the gates of Odinsdale Hall. He often thought he might glimpse Anna walking in the grounds or peeping out of one of the windows, but he never did. There was a light rain and mist made it difficult to see more than a few feet. To his surprise Raven noticed a young girl on a grey pony coming out of the gate. Raven soon surmised it was Abigail. He hadn't seen her for many years, but she was still much the same. He hurried to come alongside her and greeted her warmly. "Well, if it isn't Abigail. How are you?" said Raven.

"Oh, is that you Raven. I heard you were back. My, how you have changed. You are quite the gentleman now," said Abigail and her face coloured as she looked him up and down.

Raven smiled at this sight. The instinct predator in him knew she found him attractive, and he could turn this to his advantage.

"You are looking beautiful Abigail. You have bloomed like a Spanish flower," said Raven.

Abigail blushed even further and looked down.

"So how is Anna?" Raven said, not able to halt his curiosity about the real object of his affection.

"I'm afraid Anna is quite ill. She is in bed most of the time and Pearl looks after her. It's some kind of nervous complaint."

"Oh my God, I had no idea. And what is being done about it?"

"The doctor has given her some pills and she is to rest in bed. It's very sad. She was so full of life before."

Raven frowned and looked deep in thought. He cursed under his breath. Abigail looked uncomfortable at his bad manners.

"Is it possible for me to see her do you think?"

"No, I'm afraid Rupert wouldn't allow it. He has taken quite against you. I think he believes Anna thinks too much of you and he is jealous. He spends most of his time out and about on the estate now. He doesn't see much of Anna or even ask about her. I still dine with him in the evening, but Anna doesn't come down. He won't let anyone speak your name."

"But we mustn't let his petulance come between us Abigail. We should be friends you and me. After all, you must be lonely at the Hall, and I am lonely at Dragon Fell Farm. We can spend time together."

Abigail's face lit up with joy and she dared to look into Raven's eyes.

"Oh, Raven yes. I should like that very much."

"It's a terrible day today with this rain. Perhaps you should go back to the Hall just now. Maybe another day we could have a ride on the moor together. Do you have a telephone number?"

Anna repeated her number and her private extension that came through to her bedroom. Raven wrote it down in his notebook and put the item back in his waistcoat pocket.

"Until we meet again," Raven said and then walked swiftly away.

He smiled to himself like a cat with a mouse. Abigail watched him go with hope in her heart. She had never dared to imagine that any man would want her as she couldn't walk. She had taken comfort in being a companion to Rupert and Anna. She enjoyed the company of her dogs and the children. Yet here was a chance. Raven had grown into such a handsome man, and he seemed to have Heaven knows what riches. He would make a fine husband.

That night at dinner Abigail could not resist telling Rupert all about her meeting with Raven.

"Guess who I saw on the moor today?"

"A mongoose," said Rupert.

"No silly, Raven. He is so handsome now and he was quite the gentleman in our brief conversation."

"Abigail, I forbid you to have anything to do with that man. He is evil through and through. He would like nothing better than to wreck my family."

Tears pricked in Abigail's eyes.

"But Rupert. Anna can't help that she loves him. They were like brother and sister growing up at Dragon Fell. They have a bond. Anna loves you Rupert like a husband," she said.

"I'm not sure about that. I've seen the way he looks at her. There is more than fraternal affection in his gaze. Abigail you know nothing of the world. Evil has not been a part of your life. You must not be naïve. Raven is a bad lot. Who knows what criminal enterprises he has been involved in to make all this money he seems to have? Nobody knows his lineage. Genes will out. He is probably from a long line of tramps and thieves."

Abigail looked down and said nothing more.

That evening Abigail went in to visit Anna. Anna was pale, drifting in and out of sleep and muttering under her breath. Abigail sat quietly on a chair beside the bed.

"Anna, can you hear me? I saw Raven today on the moor. He was quite the gentleman, and we had a pleasant chat. I thought you might like to know. He wants to spend some time with me. He would like to see you, but Rupert has forbidden it. He has forbidden me too, but I was thinking I could see him in secret. What do you think?"

Hearing Raven's name seemed to rouse Anna. She sat upright and stared at Abigail.

"Raven, Raven, is he here? Is that what you said?"

"No Anna, he's at Dragon Fell. I saw him today on the moor. He asked about you," said Abigail.

"Oh, he's not here, he's not here."

"He wants to see me Anna. And you as well but Rupert won't let him. We could try to think of a way."

"Abigail! You must not see Raven alone. You must promise me. I know he is handsome with good manners now, but he is still the same underneath. He is a wolf, and you are a lamb. He will eat you alive. Stay away from him."

"Anna, how can you be so cruel? Raven wants to me my friend and I'm so lonely. You are just jealous of me."

With that Abigail fled from the room in tears.

Anna sank back down on the pillows and continued her incoherent muttering. Pearl gave her some medicine to make her sleep, but it seemed to have no effect.

Anna roused herself and sat bolt upright in bed.

"I must see Raven! I must see Raven!" she shouted.

Anna got up and opened the large window. She started to climb out of it. Pearl rushed towards her and dragged her back to the bed.

"Anna, Anna, you can't climb out of the window. You'll fall and break your neck. Come back to bed," said Pearl.

"I don't want to lie in that bed. I don't want to be alive at all. If I can't have Raven with me I don't want to be here. Oh, I hate this Hall. There is no air. I feel so crushed. I can't breathe. I want to be on the moor like when I was a girl. Remember the wind was so strong. It cleared away all your troubles. I want to be at Dragon Fell. I want to be cutting they hay with Raven and running across the fields. I want Stanley my old pony. I want to feel the wind cutting into my face. I want to be soaked by the rain. I want to feel the snow in my hands, freezing my fingertips. I can't stay here. I won't. I won't."

"Anna you mustn't talk that way. You will get well. You have everything here. Rupert loves you. In time you can go walking on the moor again. You'll see. Maybe then you could see Raven."

"Do you really think so Pearl? I would like that."

Pearl's words seem to calm her, and she sank back on to the pillows and fell asleep.

Late in the evening Abigail had sobbed herself to sleep. She felt inadequate against Anna and Rupert. Neither of them wanted her to see Raven. She wanted a special friend so much. The telephone rang and she answered it in shock.

"Hello Abigail. It's Raven."

"Oh Raven, how wonderful to hear from you. I was just thinking about you."

"How is Anna?"

"Not well I'm afraid. I told her about our meeting, but she said you were a wolf, and I shouldn't see you. She is often feverish and slips in and out of consciousness. I'm worried about her."

Raven laughed.

"I am no wolf. I have learned better manners in my years away. I have been taught how to behave by some very fine ladies in Europe. Anna is jealous of your beauty Abigail."

"Oh, do you think so? But Anna is so beautiful herself. I do love her so. It's terrible to see her now."

"I would very much like to see her. Is there a time when Rupert is not likely to be around?"

"He is out most of the day. He tends to come back for lunch and asks about Anna. Then again around eight in the evening. He goes to bed quite early and stays in his room until seven in the morning. I wouldn't risk it though Raven."

"I will think of a plan. In the meantime, you and I must become better acquainted. What about a ride tomorrow out on the moor? I could come and meet you just a few yards from the gate."

"Yes. Raven. Yes."

Abigail couldn't sleep from excitement. She wheeled herself out of her room in her dressing gown and rattled about the corridors. She decided to pop in on Anna to tell her about the phone call. Even though she wanted to see Raven she craved for Anna's approval. She also wanted Anna to know that Raven was planning to see her. She turned the knob and entered Anna's bedroom. The scene before her caused her to faint on the spot. Anna's body was on the bed wearing a white night dress. In her hand in front of her heart was a pair of sewing scissors. Blood was pooled around the scissors and was seeping on to the bed clothes. Anna's eyes were closed, and she seemed perfectly composed as if she was sleeping. Pearl was nowhere to be seen. Thunder and lightning were heard overhead, and rain poured in through the open window. The noise from the storm rose Abigail from her faint. She wheeled herself towards Anna and listened for a heartbeat. There was none. Abigail felt for a pulse. There was none. Anna's face felt as cold as snow in winter. Abigail reached for the servant bell and rang it. Pearl appeared shortly afterwards and screamed in fright. Pearl felt for a pulse but there was no beat.

"She's dead, Quite dead. Oh, the Fairbairns must be cursed. So much death."

"I will go to tell Rupert," said Abigail, her face blanched.

Pearl stood wringing her hands, feeling helpless. Rupert did not appear. Pearl gently took the scissors out of Anna's hands and mopped up the worst of the blood with a towel. She folded Anna's hands across her body and closed her eyes. Anna looked happy in death, a slight smile on her lips, her skin as white as a statue. Pearl sat with the body all night until dawn crept through the curtains. Still Rupert did not come. Pearl took it up on herself to walk down to the village. Arriving exhausted, she took the bus to town and informed the doctor and the undertaker about what had happened.

A short while later, an ambulance arrived at the Hall and took Anna's body away. Rupert had locked himself in his study and would not appear to deal with anything.

Abigail had spent the night sitting upright in bed in shock. When morning came she remembered her assignation with Raven. She could not keep it now. She telephoned to say she could not come. There was no answer. She rang and rang. Still no answer. Abigail clambered into her wheelchair and set about her morning routine. She bathed herself and dressed in a black shift dress. She had become skilled at managing her disability and she could manage most things for herself. She wheeled herself along the hall and went downstairs in the little lift that had been specially fitted for her. Then she drove into the nursery. Her tears pricked as she saw such a beautiful domestic scene before her. James and Molly were playing snap on the floor. James was laughing uncontrollably every time he got a match. Louisa was playing with some dolls on the floor, walking around between them making little sighs of delight as she arranged them into various scenarios: school lessons, weddings, beach parties with all the correct outfits.

"I'm afraid I have some terrible news for you all," said Abigail, "Anna has...died in the night."

"Died? Of what?" said Molly.

"I'm afraid it was suicide. She stabbed herself in the heart with some scissors."

Molly began to cry. Soon Abigail was doing the same. Seeing distress, soon the children joined in. They all hugged each other but could find no comfort. Abigail stayed in the nursery that morning, playing with the children quietly.

At the time of the proposed meeting, Raven rode up to the Hall, waiting for

Abigail. She did not come. The gates of the Hall were locked. Raven could see no activity within. He had the uneasy feeling something was wrong, but he couldn't put his finger on it. There was a feeling of dread that started in his heart and spread down his arms. Feeling unbearably cold, he rode back to Dragon Fell.

Chapter Seven

The next day Raven was rambling about the moor, deep in thought. He couldn't understand why Abigail had not kept their appointment. She had seemed so keen. He turned the problem over and over in his mind, but he could find no solution. It was raining lightly but Raven was snug in his waterproofs. As he climbed over a ridge and descended to the sheep track he saw a gangly lad about fourteen coming towards him. He was walking swiftly and looking furtively about him.

"Where are you off to in such a hurry?" said Raven.

"I'm going home. Quick as I can. Don't want to hang about near here."

"Whatever is the matter? The moor is safe as houses."

"You've not heard then? That lady at the Hall. Anna. She died last night. Stabbed by her own hand. They say she was haunted at the end. Possessed by demons some say. She is the type that will walk if you know what I mean. She loved the moor. I wouldn't want to meet her ghost."

"Anna. Dead. Dead you say. Dead. Where is the body?"

"I don't know rightly. Just know she is dead. I'm getting home. I'll not walk past Odinsdale Hall the day. I'm taking a shortcut over the moor. Don't want to be anywhere near the place."

With that, the boy hurried off. Raven stood in shock. His Anna dead. He strode down towards the Hall as if all the demons of Hell were at his heels. On arrival, the gates were locked. He pressed the buzzer for admittance.

"Who is it?" a voice said.

"I am Raven Fairbairn of Dragon Fell Farm. I have business with your employer. Let me in man."

The gates swung open smoothly. Raven strode towards the front door. He rapped on the door with his stick. After a few moments Mrs Harbottle appeared.

Looking flustered she asked his business. Raven looked at her with utter contempt. Pushing past her he barged into the hallway.

"Where is she? Where is Anna? Where is the body?"

Mrs Harbottle recovered enough to speak, "She's not here. Her body is in the morgue."

At that moment, Rupert burst into the hall.

"What are you doing here? You are banned from this house. You are not to set foot here again. If it wasn't for you my wife would still be alive. Get out. Get out."

Raven moved as if to strike Rupert. Then he thought better of it and turned on his heel and walked swiftly away. Beside himself with rage he did not eat nor drink that day. He wandered the moors talking to himself, bashing his head on rocks and trees. He stayed out all night in freezing rain. The creatures of the moor fled from him. Sheep ran when he came near. He fell at last and lay headlong on the bracken. He screamed Anna's name into the Earth.

"Anna, Anna, come back to me. Come to me. Haunt me. Follow me. Possess me. Do anything but don't leave me here on this Earth. I can't stay here alone."

Raven walked back to Dragon Fell and clambered into his car: a Jaguar. He drove like a madman to the morgue in town and parked outside. It was night-time now and nobody was about. He exited the car and walked around the building. He could not see a way in. Her body was in there somewhere. His Anna. What wouldn't he give to hold her one last time? The security camera lit up as Raven walked past. Even in his desperate state he knew it was too risky to break his way in. He would end up in prison and whatever happened he wasn't going to go back to one of those places again. He knelt on the pavement and bowed his head. He sent up a prayer to Anna. "My dearest Anna, I know your soul is out there somewhere. One day we will be together again. Come to me. Guide me to where you are."

There was no answer but the wind. Raven returned to Dragon Fell and collapsed into bed. He didn't get up for many days.

Anna's funeral was a strange affair. The local vicar, traditional in his views, refused to bury her in hallowed ground because of the sin of suicide. Rupert was furious but could not budge him. He found a way around. In a remote corner of the grounds of Odinsdale Hall there was an old chapel in a state of disrepair. The family had worshipped there in days of old, but it was no longer used. There was a small churchyard with some medieval graves in it and at the bottom a little gate went out on to the common land that led to the moor. Anna could be buried here. She would be a part of Odinsdale Hall but also almost on the moor. It was the perfect spot. Rupert engaged a Methodist minister for the service who was willing to officiate. The morning of the funeral was fittingly gloomy. Heavy rain poured down from a leaden sky. Anna's body was ferried from the morgue to the Hall in a black hearse. From there, the family and all the servants followed the coffin to the prepared grave just next to the gate, under the stone wall which demarcated the moor from the Hall grounds. Local dignitaries had been invited but most declined. The doctor made an appearance and the local magistrate. Rupert walked in front of the procession looking grim. Abigail, in her wheelchair, followed behind, pushed by Pearl. Pearl did not think she would ever smile again. Anna had been like a friend to her at Dragon Fell and she had rescued her when things went awry and given her a place at Odinsdale Hall. Pearl felt like she had lost her soul mate. She cried all the way to the graveside. The children with Molly stumbled along, confused about what was happening. The service was in the open air by the graveside as the old chapel was not safe to enter. The minister, grey haired, tall and stooped with age read out things from the Bible and compared Anna's life to a flower opening, blooming and dying. Rupert stepped up next to say a few words.

"I would like to say something about my beautiful Anna. I am sure she would have appreciated this open-air service as she so loved nature and particularly the moor above us. She was the light of my life and brought me so much joy. We were blessed with our perfect child Louisa. I am certain that Anna's spirit resides in Heaven where we will be reunited one day."

Rupert stepped away hiding his face as the tears came. The minister led everyone in the hymn "Abide with me" which had been a favourite of Anna's. Then he gave the final blessing and Anna's coffin was lowered into the grave. After each throwing in some earth the family walked away back to Hall for tea. Pearl wondered if Anna was really in Heaven. Some said suicides couldn't go there. Where was she then? Pearl shuddered with the thought of Anna not finding a home in the afterlife.

"Where is Mummy?" said Louisa on the way back to the Hall.

Molly could not reply. She just picked up the child and cuddled her as she walked.

Raven had roused himself enough at Dragon Fell Farm to sit at the table and drink some tea. He still could not bear the thought of food. Ben, the farm manager, was sitting opposite, warily doing some paperwork. He was afraid of Raven in this mood and was glad that his workday was soon ending.

"What news have you of the village then?" Raven said.

"Nothing that is important. I did hear that Anna is being buried today."

"Anna. Where?"

"In the grounds of Odinsdale Hall. Apparently, the vicar wouldn't bury her in the church yard. All a terrible business."

"Bastards!"

Raven slammed his fist hard on the table so that the cups jumped. He went up to his room to think.

At seven that evening Raven left the farm and walked down the hill to Odinsdale Hall. On nearing the gates, he skirted the wall and went around to the back where the gate led into the grounds. He unlatched the gate, and it squeaked open, stiff from lack of use. He saw the freshly dug grave immediately in front of him.

"Anna, Anna, oh my Anna!" he said and then let out a howl like a wolf. He lay down on the earth, covering the grave with his body. His face was pressed into the soil. Like this he could be near her. He never wanted to leave. The rain was still pouring until he was soaked through but still he lay there.

There was a squeaking sound in the distance. It was Abigail wheeling herself down to the grave. She had in her lap some of Anna's things from her bedroom. There were some shells Anna had collected from a trip to Whitby, an old childhood teddy, a lock of Louisa's hair and a little statue of an angel. Abigail planned to put them on the grave to comfort Anna. As she neared the site, she was shocked to see a figure of a man lying on the ground. She came to a stop unsure what to do. It dawned on her that this was Raven. She wheeled herself slowly forward until she was close to him.

"Raven, whatever are you doing? You are soaking. You are going to catch a cold. You must get up."

Raven raised his head slightly to look at her. She gasped when she saw his face. His pallor was unnaturally white, and his lips were bleeding from him biting them. There were gashes along his cheeks where his hands had clawed at his face. The effect was of a vampire or a goblin: some ghastly unearthly thing.

"Get up. Get up should I? I'll never get up. Everything I ever loved is in this grave. My whole world. My heart is in this grave."

"Oh Raven. You look so ill. But Anna is gone. She is in Heaven now I'm sure of it. You must learn to live again. I could help you. I could love you. You could learn to love again."

Abigail stretched out her hands towards him. Raven shot her a look of complete contempt.

"Love. Love. What do you know of love? You white faced stupid little doll. I could never love you. I would crush you to pieces. I would grind your bones to ash and throw you in the sea. I would burn you and salt the earth. I hate you and everything you are. I never loved you. I just used you to get close to Anna. She is the one I loved, not you bitch."

Abigail looked aghast. Nobody had ever spoken to her like this in her entire life. She recoiled into the back of her wheelchair in horror.

Raven advanced towards her. It seemed as if his eyes had gone completely black and his face was contorted in rage. Within seconds he was upon Abigail. He wrestled her out of the chair and flung her onto the ground. Within moments he was on top of her. Abigail was screaming at him to stop. Nobody could hear her at this remote part of the grounds. Raven was inside her, pressing on her helpless body. She screamed in pain but still it continued. After what seemed like an age Raven got up and staggered away. Abigail lay on the ground in pain. Blood trickled from between her legs. She pulled down her skirt to hide it, but she couldn't manage to get up. She just lay on the cold earth quietly whimpering. There was no sound but the crows acking to each other and Abigail could only see the grey sky above her.

"Oh my God, why do you hate me? Why are you doing this to me? Why must I always suffer?" she cried out in despair.

Hours passed and dawn broke. Thin light shone into the graveyard. Anna thought that she heard whistling. One of the old gardeners was coming along with his wheelbarrow to trim the brambles. When he saw Abigail he rushed towards her, lifted her up and set her back in the wheelchair.

"Oh Miss, whatever has happened to you? There, there. Don't take on so. Everything is all right. I'll take you back up to the Hall."

"I fell out of the chair. Just hurt myself in the fall. I'm sure I'll be all right in a while."

The gardener, old Bill, wheeled her up to the Hall, talking to her throughout, comforting her, soothing her with his voice. He had a notion that she had not told him the truth about what had happened, but he couldn't think what it could have been.

Chapter Eight

Abigail recovered in her room at Odinsdale Hall. A great fuss was made of her, and she spent many weeks in bed with Pearl and Molly taking it in turns to keep her company. She told nobody about Raven or what had really happened, and nobody asked further. The story was that in reaching down to put something on Anna's grave she had slipped and fallen out of her chair. Nothing more. In time she felt able to get up again and spend time in the library and playing in the nursery with the children. She now had a fear of going outside and wouldn't venture into the garden even on the mildest of days.

As the months passed Abigail started to put on weight. She ordered new clothes from a catalogue and said nothing about it. Her periods ceased and she felt tired more easily. Innocent as a lamb nobody had ever really told Abigail the facts of life. She had a hazy idea that she might be pregnant, but she wasn't entirely sure. She knew that Raven had raped her as she had read allusions to such things in the ancient Greek myths she enjoyed. As time went on her pregnancy became so obvious there was no hiding it anymore.

One morning Pearl was tidying Abigail's room, reaching into the corners with a feather duster and singing an old love song to herself.

"Pearl, come and sit down with me. I need to talk to you about something."

"Yes Miss Abigail. Tha knows I love to talk with thee. You are a tonic to listen to."

Pearl came and sat on the bed next to Abigail.

"Pearl, I'm getting fat and my periods have stopped. I think I'm pregnant. What do you think?"

Pearl twisted her hands in nervousness.

"I don't rightly know Miss. But I think from what you said you might be right. How though? I mean you have no husband. Who would the father be?"

"I can't tell Pearl. I can't ever tell. Please would you tell Rupert? I must tell him, but I just can't face it. Please."

"Why yes miss don't worry. I'll tell 'im directly. Everything will be all right. We'll all look after you. You just concentrate on getting strong for the baby."

Pearl exited the room and went straight to Rupert's study to tell him the strange news. Rupert's face went pale. He buried his face in his hands for several minutes. Then he recovered well.

"Thank you Pearl," he said, "Tell Abigail everything is fine. She can have the baby here. I will employ a nurse nearer the time so everything will be in order. We will carry on as normal. Don't let the servants gossip. I want you to spend all your time with Abigail. You are to look after her. Do you understand?"

"Of course, sir," said Pearl and she left the room excited at the prospect of a new baby.

Abigail rallied her spirits. Without shame she ordered maternity dresses from a London store. She spent time reading in the library or watching old films on the TV. Pearl and Abigail chatted together about everything and nothing. They were content.

In the event, there was no need for a nurse. The baby slipped into the world one fine summer morning without any fanfare whatsoever. He was a pale, sickly thing who could barely whimper. Abigail thought he looked like a bedraggled baby bird. She remembered Anna telling her she had rescued such a bird as a child. She called the baby Hawk after the bird. He didn't thrive but somehow survived. He was fussed over endlessly by Abigail, Pearl, and Molly. Rupert, morose now most of the time, glanced in on him once and then had little to do with him. He was usually in his study reading or brooding. Hawk looked like Abigail with delicate features though his skin was darker, and his hair was thick and black. He often had a cold or a fever or an upset stomach. There was always something wrong with him. Abigail worried about his health. The Dale was often cold and damp, not suitable for someone with a delicate constitution. Abigail kept him on her lap most of the time, protecting him from the world.

Autumn approached and some friends of Rupert's arrived for the shoot. They stayed in one of the cottages but dined at the Hall. Sophie, a portly lady of middle age, didn't shoot like her husband so she wandered around the Hall looking slightly bored most of the time and drinking white wine. She made a special friend of Abigail. One afternoon they were in the library. Abigail was lost in a book while Sophie was pretending to read but would much rather have been gossiping about something. The rain that day was torrential, and Sophie had no plans to go out.

"I do believe it never stops raining in this place. How do you all survive up here? It's so gloomy. Now Norfolk where I live is so much milder. Much more sunshine. It's better for the health I believe."

"We like it. I suppose we have known nothing else. I do worry about Hawk though. He is such a delicate baby. I wonder if the south would be better for his health. If anything should happen to him I don't know what I'd do. He is my world," said Abigail.

"Harold and I live on the north Norfolk coast in a place called Burnham-overy-Staithe. It's simply divine in the summer. Lots of sunshine and so much milder than here. Of course, the winter is the winter but it's much more manageable. We rarely get snow. I think you should consider moving with Hawk. It would be much better for you too. Norfolk is so flat your wheelchair would be easier to deal with."

"That sounds so lovely," said Abigail, a plan forming in her mind.

She was terrified of meeting Raven. She also worried he would find out about the baby and snatch him away.

"There's a beach and everything. We have a little boat. You can go sailing."

"Oh Sophie, do you really think it's possible?"

"Of course. I'll help you. We can be firm friends. I don't know what's got into your brother but he's not the man he was. You must be so lonely. You could bring that gawky girl to help with the baby and look after the house. There are so many darling little cottages. I'm sure we could find you something suitable."

And so, it came to be. Abigail, Hawk and Pearl moved to Norfolk just before Christmas. They had a little terraced cottage not far from the sea. Rupert paid for it all and Abigail had her inheritance to live on. She employed a wealth manager to see to her portfolio of shares. Abigail thrived without the fear of Raven. Even Hawk started to grow stronger. Pearl was in Paradise with her own little domain to look after and the child to fuss over. Abigail made a few friends, and they enjoyed coffee and cakes together.

Sixteen years passed without much event. They were a happy little family. Hawk's childhood passed in an idyllic blur. He had tutors to teach him the basics of education. Abigail thought him far too delicate for a school. He had some talent in painting and whiled away afternoons with his watercolours. He could play the piano passably. In summer, Bill, one of Abigail's friends, taught him to sail on a little yacht. They started off in the safety of the harbour and then ventured out further to the open sea. Sometimes, Abigail came along, sunning herself on the deck and drinking Pimms. They navigated through the maze of tidal creeks through the marshes. One wonderfully sunny afternoon they were out on the boat, enjoying the day. Bill took charge of the sail as Hawk preferred just to watch. Abigail was wearing a pink bathing suit and had gained some colour over the long summer. Hawk poured her another cocktail and helped himself to one.

"Hawk. You shouldn't drink. You're still a child," said Abigail.

"Oh, mum, don't be such a bore. I'm sixteen now. I'm a man. Anyway, I've put lots of lemonade in so I'm fine."

Bill halted the boat to come and join them. He put down the sail so they could drift for a while. Hawk handed him a Pimm's, and they basked pleasantly in the sun.

"Abigail, when are you going to make an honest man of me?" said Bill.

"Oh Bill, I've told you. I'm not the marrying kind. Hawk is my whole world. He is all I need," said Abigail.

"One day you'll change your mind," said Bill and kissed Abigail on the cheek.

"Who is my father? Is it your Bill?' said Hawk.

Abigail looked at him in shock. He had never asked before as if he sensed it was a delicate subject.

"That's something I don't ever want to tell you," said Abigail.

"Hawk. Just let that be. Don't upset your mother," said Bill.

Hawk rooted around in the picnic basket until he found some sandwiches. He gave one to each of them and set about eating. He didn't mention the subject again, but he was uneasy about it. His mother was so open about everything, but the origin of his birth was taboo.

"Why don't you have a swim, Hawk?" said Bill.

The sea was a perfect azure blue, and the temperature was warm after being heated through the long summer.

"No, I'm not much of a swimmer. I prefer to just sunbathe," said Hawk.

"I'm going to. See you both in a bit,"

Bill jumped off the side of the boat and swam around. Abigail took Hawk's hand as they lay side by side.

"Everything is perfect," said Abigail.

"Yes. It's always perfect when I'm with you Mum. Can I have a new model aeroplane? I've seen one I like." said Hawk.

"Of course. You can have anything you want. I love you so," said Abigail.

Bill returned to the boat, towelling himself down. He was in his fifties, grey haired but well-muscled and tanned. Abigail admired his body, but she had no wish to marry him. They sailed back to the shore without a care.

Chapter Nine

The sixteen years also passed peacefully at Odinsdale Hall. Louisa was now a young woman and James a young man. They had grown up together like brother and sister. Rupert had not sent them away to school but home educated them. His grief at Anna's death but also her perceived betrayal of him with Raven had changed him. Rupert wanted people around him and he could not risk losing anyone else. Louisa and James worked diligently at their schoolwork, but their great love was horses. They were both excellent riders and took an interest in the training of the racehorses.

Their childhood had also been perfection. It passed in a blaze of gymkhanas, pony club events, summer picnics and birthday parties. Everyone in the house doted on both and they had known nothing but kindness. As a result, they had grown up to be sunny natured and confident, convinced at the goodness of the world.

Louisa made a dashing figure as she came down to breakfast one morning already dressed for riding in jodhpurs and brown leather boots. She was wearing a tweed jacket, and her strawberry blonde hair was cut into a layered bob. Rupert caught his breath as he looked at her. He was immensely proud of her in every way. Not only was she stunningly beautiful but she was also sweet natured. She beamed at Rupert as she helped herself from the side cabinet to scrambled eggs and bacon. James was already there, a handsome boy with dark hair and huge brown eyes. He was delicately cutting up his breakfast into tiny portions before eating.

"What are your plans for today Louisa?" said Rupert.

"It's such a fine day I think I'll ride out over the moors. Maybe go up higher than usual. I want to see the view from the tops. Want to come James?"

"Of course. We could have a good gallop on the moor."

"If you are going to the high ground make sure you don't go anywhere near Dragon Fell Farm," said Rupert.

"Why ever not? Why are you so strange about that place? I've never been near enough to have a good look. But Mummy lived there as a child didn't she? I have a fascination for the place. And James was born there."

"Raven lives there still and he is an odd character. He isn't quite right in the head now people say. Some terrible things have gone on in that place. I don't want you anywhere near it. It's not safe," said Rupert.

"Don't worry. We'll avoid it," said Louisa.

Louisa and James soon departed for the stables leaving Rupert to open a thick letter he had just received. Once at the stables Louisa saddled her beautiful bay thoroughbred and James chose a black mare.

They jogged along in companionable silence. It was late August, and the moor was ablaze with purple heather. They rode up one of the little footpaths that traversed the moor.

"Let's go and look at Dragon Fell," said Louisa.

"Uncle Rupert said no," said James.

"Don't be a baby James. He will never know. Don't you want to see where you were born?"

"Yes. I do. I often think of it," said James.

Louisa trotted ahead until eventually they could see Dragon Fell Farm. They both slowed to a walk and edged closer. The farm looked quiet. No people were in evidence. It looked well-kept with neat flowerbeds and trimmed hedges. Louisa could see roses dancing in the wind.

"It's delightful," said James.

"A typical Pennine farm. But very cared for. There are no weeds on the path at all," said Louisa.

As they approached two wolf hounds sprang towards them, snarling and growling. Louisa, in shock, turned her horse and cantered away. James followed close behind. As she looked back she saw a tall, dark man appear in the doorway. She assumed it was Raven. The dogs soon gave up and loped back to the farm gate. After a safe distance, the pair stopped their horses for a rest.

"So much for seeing Dragon Fell," said Louisa, "My what fierce dogs."

"Yes. It seemed a pleasant enough place though but so windy. Imagine it in winter. So bleak," said James.

Louisa shuddered.

"Yes, the snow must be deep in winter. And it's so far from anywhere. Mummy must have been so tough to grow up there. And your father. I think this wind would make me ill,

Let's go back to the Hall," she said, and they cantered back down the hill to home.

It had been Raven at the entrance of Dragon Fell. Intrigued by the visit, he calculated it had been Louisa and James. He would have liked to get a closer look at them. He put on his coat and set off over the moor. His aim was Hobb's Crag. This had been a favourite haunt of Anna and Raven as children. It was a tall outcrop of rock with a flat top. You could see for miles from the summit. You could slide down the side of the crag and go into a small opening at the bottom. Local folk tales said if you went inside you would be given a vision of your true love. The local vicar cautioned the children from doing such a thing, but it was a popular spot with the local farmhands. Many a budding relationship had been consummated in the fairy cave. Raven climbed up the path to the top of the crag. Then he slid down to the small aperture and squeezed in. There were a few leftover candles and initials had been scratched into the rock. Raven knelt and prayed, not to God who he was not sure he believed in but to Anna or rather her soul which he very much believed still existed. He had seen Anna in dreams and visions since her death. Such occurrences had increased until they were almost daily now. She had haunted him for so many years.

"Anna, my Anna, come to me. Let me see you. I long for you. I long to be with you. How do I go where you are? Come."

He then sat down on the floor of the cave and wept. After some minutes sleep overtook him and he laid down to rest. He could not sleep much at night now and spent most nights just staring at the wall. He woke up an hour later feeling stiff. He stood up and crawled back out of the cave.

Raven climbed back up the crag top, his vision blurred from so much crying and sleeplessness. It was twilight now. The light was fading from the moor. He heard her before he saw her.

"Raven, Raven, Raven," the sound was like the moaning of the wind, but he knew it was Anna. Then her figure appeared a few yards in front of him. She was Anna but somehow lighter, almost translucent, not quite solid. She kept looking behind her as she led him on down the path, smiling at him. However fast he went, he could not catch up with her.

"Anna, Anna, wait for me," he shouted, "How do I stay with you? Where are you? What must I do to be with you?"

She didn't answer but a voice came into his head.

"Raven, I never left you. It was always you. There was no other. This is how we can be together. I nearly went to Heaven. I didn't choose the Light. I said I didn't want to go. Then I fell back down on to the moor. This is my home. It's yours too."

Then abruptly she disappeared.

Raven screamed out in anguish but however much he called her she didn't come. He trudged home again and dozed in front of the fire, his wolf hounds at his feet. His dreams were full of Anna. She was a spirit, and he was still human. It was hard for him to communicate with her. He didn't know how to bridge the gap between this world and that.

In the coming days Raven wandered the fells constantly with his dogs. He went out whatever the weather. He talked to Anna constantly, out loud. Other walkers who met him on the path gave him a wide berth. They thought him a mad man. He could hear her voice in his head and continued the conversations. As he talked to Anna more it became easier to hear her replies. He heard her voice even in dreams at night.

"Raven, Raven, come to me," she said often.

One particularly sunny day Raven woke up early. His body felt stiff. He hadn't had a bath for days so today he decided to spruce himself up. He went to the bathroom and ran the taps in his enormous claw foot bath. There was plenty of hot water and he added bubble bath from the shelf. He clambered into the steaming bath and scrubbed himself well. He felt in much better spirits than usual. His conversations with Anna meant he now knew he still had a connection with her. She was waiting for him in the other world. She would wait forever. Rupert had never meant anything to her. She had married him for money. Raven knew he himself had always been her great love. He climbed out of the bath and began shaving. He was singing an old folk song that Pearl had taught him in his youth. Then he picked out a black suit and a white shirt to wear. He looked at himself in the mirror. He was too pale and thin. Raven went downstairs and made himself some bacon and eggs for breakfast. He decided today he would need more strength. As he came to eat the food he felt a nausea, but he forced himself to continue and ate all the food. He put on his long leather riding boots and went out into the garden. It was looking glorious from all the work of John. He picked some roses from the garden. Raven went back into the house and put them in a little vase with some water. He carried his prize out down the garden path and down the moor. He enjoyed listening to the birds singing and the rabbits running away from him. The sun warmed his face. How glorious was the world and yet when you didn't have love it felt so empty. If only he and Anna could have stayed at Dragon Fell how wonderful their lives would have been.

Eventually he reached the edge of the moor and walked to the back of Odinsdale Hall. He opened the rickety gate and went straight to Anna's grave. There were some lilies in a vase in front of the headstone. Raven threw them away to the side contemptuously and replaced them with his own roses. He commenced to weed around the plot, digging up dandelions and daisies with his fingers. He then sat quietly next to the headstone.

"Anna, its' been such a long time since we have seen each other. But I feel the time is coming when we might remedy that. I feel old and stiff. The world is beautiful but there is nothing here for me now. You are all I want. It's like part of my soul is missing. I have Dragon Fell now and I'm proud of that. I wanted Odinsdale Hall as well of course. That would have stuck it to that pathetic Rupert. I can't see a way to get it now though. They have confounded me." Raven said out loud.

"Raven, Raven, you can come where I am. You just die that's all. I'll be waiting for you on the other side. It's very simple," said the voice of Anna, appearing to be real, whispering in his ear.

Raven closed his eyes and lay down on the grave. Knowing Anna's body was under the earth calmed him. He fell asleep for many hours. He woke up refreshed, feeling better than he had for months. He walked quickly back to Dragon Fell, a plan forming in his mind. All the way back he felt that Anna's spirit was with him, hovering beside him, touching his cheek, playing with his hair. Ann was beside him always.

Chapter 10

The following week everybody but Louisa seemed to be busy. Rupert and James had gone to York races to try out some young horses. Louisa had felt nauseous that morning, so she hadn't gone. She had spent the morning in bed listening to the radio and reading Horse and Hound. She had been drinking some camomile tea. By ten she was feeling so much better. She had a shower and changed into her riding clothes and went down to the stables. As usual she looked impeccable in jodhpurs, long brown leather boots and a tweed jacket. She had a chocolate brown velvet riding hat on her head. The grooms tipped their hats to her, smiling approvingly at her beauty. She decided to take Lola out, a young thoroughbred mare who was showing great promise. Lola had already been groomed and her coat shone like a conker. Louisa saddled her and slipped the bridle on easily. She led Lola out of the stable and hopped on her back with the aid of the mounting block. They jogged along the tracks of the moor admiring the heather and enjoying the feeling of the sun. Louisa had got it into her head that she wanted to see more of Dragon Fell. She turned Lola's head in that direction and toiled up the hill. The wind was keen and there was fine rain. Eventually, they reached the gates of the farm. Louisa halted, unsure of what to do next. Her mother had talked of Dragon Fell often until Louisa had become fascinated with the place. Louisa remembered her mother talking about hay making and Christmases with mince pies and sherry. She had told Louisa about long walks and rides with Raven over the Fells. Anna looked at the windows and tried to work out which bedroom would have been her mother's.

Just as she was about to leave, thinking that her journey had been silly, Raven appeared at the door and saw her. He waved and started walking towards her down the front path. Louisa waved back. On reaching her, Raven patted Lola confidently and looked her over.

"That's a fine beast you've got there," said Raven.

"Thank you so much. Yes. I love her. I'm Louisa," she said and put out her hand. Raven took it and shook it.

"You will know me no doubt. I'm Raven. I was a great friend of your mother's many years ago."

"Yes. She talked of you often."

"Would you come inside and take some tea. I am lonely here these days."

Louisa, in her innocence, could see no harm and she readily agreed. She dismounted and Raven led Lola round to the stables at the back. Louisa followed him and they entered the farm through the back door. The house was empty other than the wolf hounds who were dozing by the fire. Louisa reached out to them, and they let her stroke them, seeing that she was no foe.

Raven asked her to sit near the fire where it was warm, and she took off her leather riding gloves. The old house had a cold feeling inside, even in August. Anna looked around, admiring everything. It was clean and there was heavy wooden furniture in the kitchen area. There was an old black range, but new kitchen units had also been fitted with marble tops. There were two well stuffed armchairs near the fire and then a huge leather sofa further out in the room. Louisa wondered what was in the many polished cabinets and cupboards she could see lining the walls. Raven watched her admiringly for a few moments. He then busied himself making the tea as there were no assistants to be seen. He brought in the tea tray and some little cakes made of sponge with buttercream topping them. They sat for a while looking at each other. Raven was drinking her in. He could see some of Anna in her but then the effect was ruined by her also having too much of Rupert. She was more delicate looking than Anna and her face had a natural haughtiness just like Rupert's. Raven had to concentrate to stop himself recoiling in disgust at this thought.

"So, tell me all about life at Odinsdale Hall," Raven said.

"We are very happy there. I learn things from books at home and so does James. We spend a lot of time together. We are both horses mad. We are mostly riding or training the racehorses or some such thing. We have so much fun," said Louisa.

"How delightful. And what of Rupert? How is he these days?"

"Papa is a treasure. He spends most of his time with the racehorses, and in the evenings he reads in the library. Of course, he has been sad since Mummy died, but he keeps busy. He really is the most perfect father."

"And his health?"

"Very well I think. He certainly never complains about anything."

"Splendid. You now Louisa, you are a young woman now. What are your plans? Are there any boyfriends on the horizon?"

"No! I don't really think of that. I love being at the Hall with Papa and James. I don't think of anyone else. I sometimes receive invitations to parties and things, but I don't usually go. I'm not that sort of person. I like my horses and I love to read. Riding on the moor is my favourite thing in the world. I am content."

"You have some of your mother in you then. She loved the moor and reading. She was an excellent rider and completely fearless. She knew a little bit about everything from books."

"Yes. I have heard. You grew up with Mummy didn't you?"

"Indeed, I did. I was an orphan you see, brought to the farm by your grandfather. Anna and I spent all our time together. We rode and walked for miles every day. We knew every inch of this moor. I loved her more than I have ever loved any human. I left though because there was bad feeling between your uncle Philip and me. That was the hardest day of my life. I hoped to reconcile with Anna when I came back. Her death was a terrible thing. I don't think I will ever recover from the loss."

"That is incredible. Such strong love. Mummy talked of you often. I think she loved you as much as you loved her."

"I hope that's true," said Raven, "but people didn't like me you see, on account of me being an orphan. They all thought I wasn't good enough for Anna. When the old man died, I was treated like a servant. I probably had poor origins, no breeding."

At this moment Anna thought he might be about to cry.

"I'm sure that's not true. You seem to have a gentlemanly bearing. I can imagine you had a regal past. Perhaps you were an Indian prince or a Maharajah. I can see you with golden turban and clothes of fine silk, dripping in gold and wearing an enormous emerald necklace. You were out sailing one day when a ship of evil pirates appeared and spirited you away. You found yourself in England after a long sea journey but when you reached land you ran away from the ship in the middle of the night. You were wandering around the docks of London, but nobody could understand anything you said. Then grandpapa found you and took you in. The rest is history."

"That's a fine story Louisa. I would like to think it was true. I made myself into a gentleman eventually," said Raven.

"How did you make your money?" said Louisa.

"That's a long story, maybe better for another day. I did many things and travelled to all kinds of places. I did some things I'm not proud of, but I got what I wanted in the end. Dragon Fell Farm. I always had that ambition and I achieved it," said Raven.

Louisa noticed how thin Raven was and how drawn his features were. He seemed to have a sad, faraway look and his eyes seemed to glisten. She saw how he seemed to shiver from time to time and his skin was clammy. She wondered if he was unwell but was too polite to ask.

"I am lonely here Louisa. I would like it if you would visit more."

"Yes. I would like to. The farm is quite delightful. But I must be getting back. Everyone will be wondering where I am."

With that, she put her gloves back on and left. Riding home on Lola she felt a wave of elation. She had made a new friend in Raven, and she had had an adventure all on her own. She was proud of herself. She decided to say nothing about the visit to Rupert or James. It would be her secret. Even though she had enjoyed herself, she had a slight uneasiness about Raven. He certainly seemed ill and almost as if he wasn't quite in this world. She remembered her mother had love him so much surely that meant he couldn't be as bad as her father said. Maybe Papa was just jealous of him. He was certainly a handsome man in a completely different way to the men of her own family.

That night in bed Louisa pored over the old photos of her mother that were kept in an album. There weren't very many from early childhood. She noticed that some of them looked as if they had been cut, as if a person had been removed. Louisa realised that it would be Raven, erased from memory by her father. The later photos were all the time Anna had spent at the Hall, smiling photos with Rupert. Louisa fell asleep with the album in her hand.

Chapter Eleven

One dinner time at the Hall, Louisa and James came into the dining room in high spirits. Their horse had won at the local races giving them a great boost. They both sat down at the table, smiling with shining faces. James helped himself to some bread and butter that had already been placed in the centre of the table and nibbled at it.

"What an amazing day. Papa you should have been there. Martell ran like the wind. It was so exciting. I thought she would be beaten but she pulled it all out at the last minute," said James.

"I was so proud. Everyone's hard work paid off. I felt like we all had a stake in it," said Louisa.

She laughed gaily and started humming a tune from a current pop song. She suddenly noticed Rupert had an unusual sombre expression.

"Why Papa, what on earth is the matter?" said Louisa.

"I'm afraid I have received some sad news. My sister Abigail, your Aunt, has sadly died. She had been suffering from cancer for some time, but she had not told me. Her son Hawk is all alone in the world now. I must look after him. I will need to go down to Norfolk to see to the arrangements. I think Abigail should be buried here in the church yard. I will have her body brought back for the funeral."

"I'm so sorry," said James.

"Papa, I am sorry too," said Anna.

They all embraced each other, giving comfort. The rest of the evening was spent sitting quietly in the drawing room, reading and occasionally talking in hushed tones. Rupert reminisced about his childhood with Abigail and how happy they had been. He had a couple of whiskies to steady his nerves. Rupert thought Abigail had had a rough lot in life. First, not being able to walk, then the unplanned pregnancy and the sickly child. Now cancer had got her. He didn't understand how God could let this happen when people like Raven were still walking around on the Earth.

The following day, Louisa slunk away on her own and set off on foot for Dragon Fell. She felt that Raven should know the news about Abigail somehow. It was Autumn now and the wind was becoming cold. The trees were turning brown and beginning to lose their leaves. They were putting on a show of russet red, purple and amber in a last hurrah. Beneath her feet, the fallen leaves crunched soothingly. A light rain started, and the wind increased the higher she climbed up the Fell. At one point she saw a buzzard hovering over his prey just a few yards in front of her. After two hours of walking Louisa arrived at the gates of Dragon Fell. She walked up the path and knocked at the door with the old gargoyle knocker. Raven answered and beckoned her inside. They sat as before in front of the roaring log fire, drinking tea and eating shortbread. Yet again there appeared to be nobody else in the house.

"So, what brings you here today looking so sombre?" said Raven.

"I have sad news. My Aunt Abigail has died. Rupert is going down to organise her affairs. She is to be buried in the church yard. Her son Hawk is coming to live with us. Her life has been so sad."

"I'm sorry to hear this. Do you know Hawk is my son?"

Louisa's face blanched in horror.

"What? How can that be? You were never married to her, were you? Nobody ever told us who Hawk's father was."

"You must understand it is not necessary for marriage for babies to happen. Let's just say that Abigail and I had a short liaison and Hawk was the result."

"I see. That kind of explains some things that never really made sense to me."

"Indeed. I have a mind to see Hawk. He is my son. Perhaps he could keep me company here. Maybe you and he will grow to like each other. Maybe even marry. But, no I am being a foolish old man. Girls these days make their own matches."

"What a strange notion. I don't know. I've never met Hawk or even seen a picture of him. I don't think I'm ready for a relationship. I don't think about marriage. I just like being with James and Papa."

"Yes. I'm sure you are very comfortable there. Everything is easier at Odinsdale Hall. Much milder weather and grander surroundings. I had a notion to buy it for myself at one time. Make Rupert an offer he couldn't refuse. But that's all finished with now. I haven't the strength anymore," Raven said.

"I often think of marrying James, but he is my cousin. Maybe that's not allowed. I'm not sure," Louisa said.

"People marry their cousins all the time. I saw it in India and Pakistan. It keeps the money in the family you see. That's why they do it," said Raven.

"Tell me about my mother. What was she like as a child? I would love to know all about the time she lived here," said Anna.

"Your mother was the most beautiful woman that ever lived. She could ride any horse, shoot a shotgun, walk for miles. She had a fearless spirit and would speak up to anyone. She had the most gorgeous auburn hair that I have never seen the like of except in old paintings. It was as if she was a goddess on Earth. We spent all our time together as little children, rain or shine, we'd be out on the moor looking at the animals and birds. When I look back it always seemed to be summer, and the sun shone on the purple heather."

Louisa noticed a tear in the corner of his eye. She no longer felt so comfortable with Raven after his revelation about Abigail. Louisa made her excuses and left. She hurried back down the hill frowning. The rain was heavier now, and the paths were a sea of mud. The world was darker than she had thought.

On arrival at the Hall, she had a bath and changed out of her muddy clothes. The hot water calmed her. She dressed in a cashmere sweater and a kilt and went to sit in the drawing room with an herbal tea. She scooped up Fergi, the little corgi, on to her lap to pet. James came in.

"You've been out a long time. I was getting worried about you."

"I just went for a walk on the moors to clear my head. It's so awful about Aunt Abigail. It's just made me feel so strange. Did you ever hear who Hawk's father was?"

"No. I didn't ever understand that."

"Nor me. I suppose we shouldn't ask Papa. Maybe it's something best not to know."

"I think you are right. There is something fishy about Hawk's birth," said James.

"Can women have children without being married?" asked Louisa.

"Of course, they can. It happens all the time. Haven't you been paying attention to the books we read in English Literature? It just like horses. Some women just do it once with a man and it happens though they never meant it. Some women get raped. These days there are lots of people who don't bother to get married at all. They just live as if they are. You are so naïve Louisa," said James.

"What is rape?" asked Louisa.

"It's when a man forces himself on a woman without her consent. It's a terrible thing. It's not good for you to dwell on such things," said James.

"It makes me squirm to think of it. Aunt Abigail might have been raped. How horrible for her," said Louisa?

"Your imagination is running away with you. You don't know that's what happened. Nobody knows. Just let sleeping dogs lie. Come on, let's find something good to watch on tele," said James.

A few days later Rupert appeared back at Odinsdale Hall with Hawk. They arrived in the drawing room together. Louisa regarded Hawk with amazement. He had no hint of Abigail in him now. He had thick black hair that was hanging long on his shoulders, cut bluntly into a bob like a girl. He was wearing dark blue jeans and a black shirt. The thing that was most striking about him was his incredible thinness. He looked like a breath of wind would blow him away and his skin was so pale he was almost translucent. He was wearing thick spectacles which enlarged his dark brown eyes.

"These are your cousins Hawk. Louisa and James. I'm sure you are all going to be great friends," said Rupert.

"I'm very pleased to meet you both," said Hawk in a high reedy voice.

"Welcome to Odinsdale Hall," said Louisa.

"Yes welcome. You will be well looked after here," said James.

"I'm afraid I feel tired after my journey. Could I be shown to my room?" said Hawk.

Mrs Harbottle was sent for and showed Hawk up to his quarters leaving James and Louisa to look at each other in shock at the strange boy. He did not appear for the rest of the evening and had his dinner sent up to his room. Pearl had also come back with him and made herself comfortable in her old room. She was glad to be back. Though Norfolk had a mild climate she had always longed to be back in Odinsdale. It was a part of her somehow and she would be happy to end her days in the Pennines where she had been born.

***

The funeral was as grim as funerals always are. There was a dull church service in the village and then Abigail was laid to rest in the church yard near to her parents and all the other Fitzwilliams that had lived out their days at Odinsdale Hall. In time her gravestone was brought to grace the spot: a pretty pillar with an angel blowing a trumpet at its top. Hawk could barely stand during the service and had to lean on James for support. He seemed incredibly physically weak. They all want back to the Hall for a funeral tea. Mrs Harbottle, Pearl and Molly bustled about serving everyone tea and biscuits. All the local gentry had been invited and most came. After the tea whisky and wine was served. A tall, broad farmer's son from lower in the Dale tried to engage Louisa in conversation. She smiled politely, barely understanding his strong Yorkshire accent. As he spoke she surveyed the local men. She could not imagine marrying any one of these specimens. They were either too thin or too broad and none of them seemed over-burdened with brains. Her eyes wandered to James who was deep in conversation with the local vet, talking about Monday morning disease. He was the most handsome man in the room. His dark hair shone, and his skin was the colour of an old pine chest. He had filled out to be muscular but didn't have surplus fat on his body. Louisa wanted him even though they were cousins. She was not sure if it would ever be possible.

***

Hawk settled in at the Hall. Despite his infirmity, he walked down to the church yard every day to lay flowers on his mother's grave and then hobbled back. The exertion was too much for him so he would spend recovery time lying in bed. He missed his mother like an ache. She had indulged his every whim and spent nearly all her time with him. Now he felt completely alone in the world. He found the Pennines to be cold and bleak and he didn't like his new family. Everyone seemed so busy with their own lives they didn't have time to bother with him. Louisa and James were horse mad, but Raven couldn't see the appeal. Rupert seemed to be always in his study and had barely spoken two words to him. Hawk was in terrible health. He spent most of his days in bed coughing and wheezing, complaining about one thing or another. He treated Pearl as his personal slave. He was constantly ringing the internal telephone down to the kitchen, asking for tea to be brought up, or sweets, or cake. He watched television in his room or read comic books. He couldn't bear the dogs to be near him as their hair made him sneeze. He wouldn't have the windows open as he disliked the smell of manure and horses. Louisa and James tired of his company quickly and left him to his own devices. They carried on with their lives of racehorses and walks just as before. Mrs Harbottle called the doctor to examine Hawk. Nothing much came of the visit other than a diagnosis of chronic fatigue for which there was no cure. He also had a weak heart.

Louisa did not return to Dragon Fell Farm now Hawk was in residence at the Hall. She kept her knowledge of his fatherhood secret. She was uneasy about Raven and his intentions for the boy. It was a good thing Hawk was so sickly as he was unlikely to meet Raven rambling on the moor. His idea of her marrying Hawk seemed so ridiculous now she had finally met her cousin. He wasn't her idea of a man. She wondered why Raven had wanted that. A thought occurred that it was a match to make money or some strange revenge on Rupert. These dark thoughts were kept from Louisa's mind by busy days with the horses. She threw herself into the racehorse business and talked to nobody but James.

Chapter Twelve

Raven, disappointed that Louisa had never returned, wandered on the moor daily. He went close to Odinsdale Hall some days in the hopes of seeing Louisa, but he never did. Even the animals seemed wary of Raven. The birds kept their distance, and he didn't see any owls in the trees, only heard their hooting. The rabbits did not come out to play in front of him and the foxes stayed in their lairs. He was totally alone. One cold day he met Molly on one of the sheep tracks.

"Molly. How are you? Still here in Odinsdale. I thought you would be long gone. Are you still at the Hall?"

"Yes, I like it there. Louisa and James are virtually grown now but I still help. I'm general dogsbody."

"And Abigail's child. Is he there now?"

"Hawk. Yes. He's always ill. Quite hard to deal with. He keeps Pearl run off her feet."

"I see. Well good to see you. I must be gone."

He turned down a track to the side and walked quickly away. Raven turned over the news in his mind, but he could see no way of achieving his aims. Nothing would have given him greater pleasure than to be the master of both Dragon Fell and Odinsdale Hall, but he was failing now. A marriage between Hawk and Louisa had been on his mind but it didn't seem likely. Louisa looked like a girl who knew her own mind. Raven coughed in the mornings and his mind couldn't seem to hold a train of thought for more than a few moments. He felt an incredible fatigue as if a great weight was on his body. Raven's mind was mostly full of Anna. He dreamed about her each night. As he went to sleep she was in his thoughts and as he woke up there she was again. He walked the moors day and night calling to her. Sometimes he thought he caught a glimpse. Sometimes she appeared before him, always just out of reach, leading him on.

One grim night it was raining hard. Raven was in bed and couldn't sleep. He stared at the wall, brooding. He thought he heard his name being called from outside the window. Maybe it was just the wind. He opened the casement to look but he couldn't see anything but blackness. He could still hear the voice. He put on his clothes and boots and went outside. The voice was louder now, calling him through the rain and the wind. He kept on and on.

"Anna, Anna, wait for me. Let me be with you."

He could see her better now. She was a few feet in front of him, a beautiful young woman as she had been, but lighter, translucent and she seemed to hover in front of him. He kept trudging on behind her, wanting more than anything to be where she was. Hours and hours he seemed to wander on the moor, not knowing where he was. It rained and it rained. His hair was plastered to his head, his feet were soaked through. Still, he kept on. Following. He arrived at Hobb's Crag and toiled along to the top where the stone flattened out. There Anna was, hovering in front of him.

"Come Raven. Come. Follow me to Paradise."

She beckoned him towards her, all the while seeming to hover in the air. He stepped forwards and then there was no more rock. He had stepped off the crag. He plunged down to the bottom of the outcrop where the fairy cave was. His body lay, mangled and bloody on the sodden ground. It lay there for many days. Nobody had missed him. Nobody knew he was there.

A week later he was found by a sheepdog passing by with an old shepherd from one of the tenant farms. The old man, still strong despite his years, hoisted Raven's body onto his back and carried him down to the village. From there he was taken to the morgue in town. A letter was found among his belongings asking to be buried on the moor. Nobody agreed to this request. The vicar refused to officiate anywhere at all as Raven had never been christened, never been near a church in his life and had a reputation for wickedness. The Reverend Thomas Whinstone spent most of his time at home in his comfortable vicarage, poring over obscure parts of the Old Testament, planning dull sermons about arcane points of scripture that nobody understood. He was the gatekeeper of Heaven and had done his best to keep Anna and Raven out. Nobody knew how he justified to his Christian spirit damning the souls of others to eternal Hell. Perhaps one day he would need to explain his actions to his Maker. In the end Raven was cremated. Only John, Ben and Pearl attended.

One frosty morning saw John and Ben toiling down from Dragon Fell Farm to the back of Odinsdale Hall. They carried Raven's ashes in a small black urn. The frost had turned the moor into a magical fairy land. Spider's webs were glistening on the blackthorns and the turf was transformed into a carpet of silver. The two men walked on in silence. Eventually, they reached the little gate at the back of the Hall. Anna was buried just a few feet away in the grounds of the

Hall. The moor petered out here and the manicured gardens of Odinsdale Hall began. The moor had a way of inveigling itself into the garden. The heather spread through the gateway and into the old cemetery. Bracken and brambles had started to take over against the wall and were wandering through the graves. Nettles sprung up everywhere.

"He would have wanted to be near Anna I think, but I daren't scatter him in the old graveyard. If I'm caught the toffs will have plenty to say I'm sure," said John.

"Aye, you're right. He loved Anna more than anybody had ever loved another. He was never right after she died. It makes you think. What about scattering him just here, near the gate? Then he's kind of with her like," said Ben.

"That's the idea. Give him here," said John, taking the urn from Ben.

He reached in and started throwing some of the ash around. Ben did the same until there was only a little left in the bottom.

"Do you think we should say some words?" asked Ben.

"Aye we better," said John.

He cleared his throat.

"Here lies Raven. He was a creature of the moor, and this is the right place for him to be. He was a wild thing just like the kestrels and hawks and just as pitiless. Let's hope he rests in peace in the hope of the resurrection," said John.

"Amen," said Ben.

John walked back to the gate and opened it gingerly.

"I want to put the rest of him on Anna's grave. It's what he would have wanted. Keep a look out and I'm going to take him to her," he said.

He walked through the gate and towards Anna's headstone. There were some roses lying in a little vase. John placed the urn down in front of the roses and bowed his head.

"There you are you old bastard. You are both together now. You got what you wanted in the end," he whispered.

The two men walked back up to Dragon Fell to feed the beasts saying not a word to each other.

***

Death also came to Odinsdale Hall that month. Rupert had been more and more morose as the years went by. He lost interest in the racehorses and spent most of his time shut up in his study. He read books endlessly and stared into the fireplace. He couldn't understand how his life had turned to bleakness when he thought he had done everything right. He had tried to be a good man. He had treated his employees well. He had loved Anna as best as he was able, but her heart had always belonged to someone else. Now he was alone apart from Louisa the only joy of his life. Even the thought of his daughter couldn't cheer him now. He had started to take more whisky in the evenings than was good for him. One cold evening he was sitting in front of the study fire as usual. There was a copy of an Old Brontë novel in his hands. He was trying to read but the print seemed incredibly small to his ageing eyes. As he read the words became more and more blurred. He felt a pain deep in his chest and down his arm. It was so sharp he cried out in agony. Then his breath just seemed to stop. The book fell from his hands and his head lolled back in the chair. After a few moments something of a smile seemed to take over his face. In a few minutes Pearl came in to close the curtains. She found him just like this, seeming at peace.

"Oh Mr Fitzwilliam, not you as well. Oh, whatever is the matter here? Another death. I have lost nearly everyone," said Pearl and she dropped to her knees and wept.

Rupert was buried with great pomp and ceremony in the churchyard with his family, not in the old chapel cemetery with his wife. The decision caused something of a stir in the district. The old gossips had plenty to say about it. The morning of the funeral Louisa woke with a feeling of dread in the pit of her stomach. The death of her beloved father was the first terrible thing to happen in her charmed life. She couldn't imagine life without Papa. He had always been there, steering the ship of her life, giving advice, showering her with every comfort. Louisa showered and put on a plain black dress she had bought for the occasion. She stepped into some black stilettoes and went down for breakfast. James was already there, looking ill at ease. Hawk had yet to appear. Louisa doled out some kedgeree and picked at it rather than eating it with her usual heartiness. James was making do with black coffee as he had no appetite. "I don't know how to make it through the day," said Louisa.

"We will. We'll make it together. Just keep your head up and smile. Think of the good times. Remember all those lovely Christmases. That's what we hold on to," said James.

"Yes. And I hope Papa is in Heaven with Mummy. They can be together," said Louisa.

"Of course, he will be looking down on us. He wouldn't want us to be upset. We must live our lives like he would have wanted," said James.

Mrs Harbottle appeared to take away the breakfast things.

"I'm afraid Hawk won't be joining you at the funeral. He feels too ill," the housekeeper announced.

Louisa and James pretended to be disappointed but in fact they were not. They both went to sit in the morning room until they were called to go to the funeral cars. Mrs Harbottle bustled in and announced that everything was ready for them. They walked out to the car together. Louisa had on a sable coat to keep out the sharp wind. It had originally belonged to her grandmother. She had found it at the back of a wardrobe, long neglected. She was glad of it as the day was bitter and she felt it even on the short journey from the door to the car. The car followed the funeral carriage to the church. Rupert's coffin was in a black horse drawn carriage. The horses had black feathers on their bridles and a man with a top hat and cane walked in front of them. It was the full works kind of a funeral. Progress was slow but the cortege eventually arrived at the little village church. Men from the estate carried the coffin inside. The church was packed with everyone from Odinsdale paying their respects. Louisa surveyed everyone and realised that she had no real connection with the people of the Dale. She hardly knew them in fact. She held on tight to James' hand, feeling like he was all she had left in the world. The vicar did a reasonably good job of the service, describing Rupert's life and works in glowing terms. Then they all trooped out to the graveyard. Seeing the coffin being lowered into the earth it hit Louisa that she would never be with her father again, at least in this life. She threw some earth on the coffin lid, and they all went back to the Hall for a grim funeral tea. After a warming glass of whisky Louisa made her excuses and left. She couldn't bear to make polite conversation with all those dull people.

She crept upstairs and threw off her clothes. Then she poured a hot bath and put plenty of bubble bath into the water. Lying in the warmth, she felt better. She pictured her father in her mind and sent all the love she had towards him. She hoped he was happy in Heaven.

***

Raven had made no will that could be found. After some legal wrangling his estate fell to James as the closest living relative, though the truth was that Raven had no true blood relatives. James inherited Dragon Fell Farm and a substantial fortune locked in the vaults of Coutts and Co in London. There were shares and investments, gold bars, oil paintings and jewellery. James was a wealthy man. Louisa inherited Odinsdale Hall and all of Rupert's business interests. They were the richest people in the Dale by a long way.

***

Hawk was fading fast. He spent all his time in bed now, propped up on his pillows watching television or listening to the radio. He didn't like anything about Odinsdale Hall, and he missed his mother terribly. He dreamed of the carefree days in Norfolk on the little yacht, basking in the summer sunshine. He remembered fondly the little tea shop in the local town where his mother took him for cream cakes after shopping trips. On this particular cold morning he pulled the bell cord for Pearl. She appeared within a few minutes.

"Pearl. I am cold. Will you please have the heating turned up? I also want some logs on the fire. And a hot chocolate. I must have a hot chocolate," said Hawk.

"Yes of course Master Hawk. Whatever you want."

She piled some logs on to the bedroom fireplace and make kindling out of newspaper balls. She lit the fire expertly due to long practice. Then she disappeared to make the hot chocolate.

Hawk was shaken by a coughing fit that lasted several minutes. He pulled the duvet cover further around himself and switched on the television. He liked to watch just about anything. There was an Australian soap opera on, and he settled down to enjoy it. Pearl came in with the hot chocolate and gave it to him. He spooned it little by little into his mouth, spilling some of it on the duvet cover.

"What about a nice walk Hawk? It would do you good. We could use the old wheelchair. I could push you around the garden. Fresh air is a tonic," said Pearl.

"No Pearl, I am far too tired now for that kind of thing. My body feels so heavy. I have aches and pains all over. I miss Mummy. I want my Mummy. What is the point of me living without her? I can't see the way forward," said Hawk.

Pearl sat on the bed and took Hawk's face between her hands.

"You must not talk like that Hawk. You will get well. You are so young. You have your whole life. Maybe even one day you'll meet a girl and get married," said Pearl.

"Humf! I don't like girls. I don't want to be married," said Hawk.

"Concentrate on getting well. I'm going down to the kitchen to make you some chicken soup. That will make you strong," said Pearl.

Off she went at her wit's end with what to do with Hawk.

Later in the evening, Hawk worsened. He was now running a fever. One moment he was hot and the next he was complaining of chills. He wouldn't eat but just lay on the pillows moaning softly. Pearl tried to spoon soup and tea into his mouth. Outside there was a blizzard. Snow was falling heavily and there was a high wind whistling through the window casement. Pearl called the doctor, but he refused to come, saying the weather was too bad. He advised keeping Hawk warm with lots of fluids. Pearl sat with him through the night as he wailed and moaned. Dawn came creeping through the window and the wind finally dropped. Hawk was no better. He was now struggling to breathe, choking and wheezing. He seemed only half conscious, drifting in and out of sleep. By the afternoon, Hawk's skin had started to turn blue. Pearl was beside herself. She phoned the doctor again who said he would come as soon as he was able. It was too late. Two hours later, Hawk was dead. Pearl closed his eyes and sat silently by the bed. She struggled to make sense of Hawk's life. He had always been a difficult child, not strong enough to live in the world. Why had he ever been born? The doctor gained admittance and declared Hawk to have died of influenza after a brief examination. Pearl glared at the doctor but said nothing. She thought if he hadn't been so fond of his own comfort he may have been able to save Hawk.

Another funeral took place. Hawk's funeral procession was like a mini version of Rupert's. Out again came the black carriage and the horses with the dark feathers. Again, the man in the top hat and the cane walked in front of the carriage. There was the same vicar, the same church and the same churchyard. Hawk was buried next to his mother. The church was not so full this time with just a handful of mourners. Hawk had made no friends in Odinsdale. Pearl comforted herself that at least now he was with Abigail. Hopefully, everyone was there together in the other world. She had tried her best to love Hawk, but he had made it so terribly difficult. If Pearl was honest, there was almost a sense of relief at his passing.

***

Louisa did not shed many tears for Hawk. She went back to her previous life of horses and moorland rides. She was mistress now of Odinsdale Hall and she was loving every minute of it. She managed the house affairs from Rupert's old study in the mornings and in the afternoons she threw herself into managing the racehorse business. She was always out, supervising the training or off to horse sales or race meetings. She received endless invitations to parties which she never attended. Young hopeful men would telephone to ask her to dinner or to a ball. She had no interest in any of them. Her heart belonged to James. They had never spoken of it, but their bond was strong. James accompanied Louisa on her racehorse business, spent evenings with her reading or watching television. They had the kind of relationship that did not need words. They found comfort in each other's presence. They knew what the other wanted without asking.

One morning Louisa was in the study opening letters and skim reading them. Pearl was dusting around her.

"Pearl, is James my cousin?"

"Well of course he is miss. James' mother was Kanshi, but his father was Philip. Philip was your mother's brother so yes you are cousins."

"Are cousins allowed to marry?"

"I don't rightly know. I think there have been cases of it yes. But people don't usually do it."

"Why don't they?"

"I think the children, well, they might not be right you know. Have things wrong with them when the blood's too close."

Louisa shuddered.

"Ugh!" she said.

"Why do you ask about such things?"

"One day I am supposed to marry. Carry on the Fitzwilliam line and all that. But I don't like any of the men I meet. I want to marry James."

"Oh my. That would be something. I'm not sure about it. You best ask someone cleverer than me,"

"Pearl, you have the most common sense of anyone in the Hall. I trust your judgement more than anyone."

Pearl blushed and carried on with her dusting, slightly troubled by Louisa's idea. Louisa got up in a rush and stomped down the hall to find James. He was watching television in the drawing room, laughing at a comedy show. "

James we need to have a day out. Spend quality time together. Why don't we go to Whitby?" said Louisa.

"Whitby? Well, why not? I haven't been for ages. Splendid idea," said James.

They changed their clothes and James had the men bring round the old MG to the front of the house. It was early spring, but the sun was shining. They hopped into the vintage car with the top down and sped off to the coast. On arrival in the old fishing town James parked the car and then they walked along arm in arm admiring the scenery. There was a keen wind, but it didn't bother them. They both loved the old fishermen's houses with their red tiles rooves. They climbed up to the ruins of the Abbey and sat down among the stones for a rest.

"I've been thinking," began Louisa, "we get on well you and me. We know everything about each other, and we never argue."

That's true. What on earth are you driving at?" said James.

"We should get married and be together forever. I've looked around and nobody else interests me. Will you marry me James?"

"But we are cousins. People say you shouldn't marry your cousin."

"Who says? People. Stuff people. We are ideal for each other. Marry me James. What say you?"

James laughed.

"Yes my crazy Louisa. Yes. Yes. I will."

He reached over and kissed her, and they stayed in a locked embrace for many minutes.

"That's that sorted then. If we have strange babies we will just have to deal with it. I'm sure Pearl and Molly could manage an oddity between them. Come on, let's get back and tell everyone."

With that they wended their way back to the car arm in arm.

The wedding was not a grand affair. Louisa and James decided they couldn't bear any fuss and they didn't want to deal with the scandalised faces of the local gentry. They booked a holiday to Barbados to get married abroad. The flight was long and uncomfortable, and it made Louisa regret their decision. Once safely ensconced in the beautiful hotel she felt better. There was a private beach and several restaurants and bars in the complex. They had a few days to decompress before the big day. These days were spent lounging on the beach and sipping cocktails. They both were sunburnt after the first day, not used to sunny weather. They curled up together in their large hotel bed but Louisa rebuffed James' advances and said she wanted to save herself for her wedding night.

The big day arrived. Louisa wore a simple white dress of silk, and the hotel provided a large bouquet of flowers. James was in a beige linen suit, feeling ridiculously hot. The marriage took place on the beach with several local officials and a photographer. While exchanging their rings, a group of local youths appeared in the background on a rubber dinghy shouting obscenities at them. It rather ruined the effect. A wedding in a tropical paradise wasn't quite as beautiful as the holiday brochures made out. Afterwards they walked along the beach and had a wedding breakfast that had been laid out for them on a table with the waves lapping at their feet. James suffered from insect bites on his legs that irritated him for the rest of the holiday.

That evening James managed to perform the deed admirably, and the marriage was consummated. Louisa laid back on the pillow afterwards feeling contented that the whole thing had been achieved. She was secretly disappointed that sex was not as mysterious or earth shattering as she had thought it might be.

"It's just like horses isn't it?" said Louisa.

James dissolved into fits of laughter and kissed her on the forehead.

"Yes, my love. It's just like horses," said James.

Exactly nine months later a baby was born to James and Louisa at Odinsdale Hall. Louisa had an easy home birth without any fuss. She was back supervising her racehorses the very next day. Arabella arrived in the world in perfect health. She was as stunning as her mother and became the darling of everyone in the place in no time at all. Her hair was all blonde curls, and her chubby limbs and wide smile charmed all the estate workers.

***

James had no reason to live at Dragon Fell Farm or even to visit it. It stood empty for many years, sliding into decay. The decision was made to sell it. A young couple from London turned up one day. They were called Linda and Giles. Giles had his own woodworking company and worked from home. He made all kinds of ornaments and cabinets out of wood.

They sold for a fortune in London galleries. Linda wrote romance novels. They had a little child called Noah. They set about renovating and modernising. The farm was now bright and cheerful with natural wooden furniture and Swedish sofas. Vegetables grew in the garden and southern European varieties found a home in the huge polytunnel that Giles erected. Friends from the big city came to visit most weekends and the farm rang out with laughter as they all partied together.

One bright morning, Noah was playing in the garden. Following a butterfly, he wandered out of the front gate on to the moor. Oblivious to his surroundings, he meandered along. He stopped to admire a buzzard hovering far above him. He was distracted by the white rumps of two little rabbits, so he chased them until they hid from him in their burrows. Noah sat down on a clump of heather to rest. It was then that he saw a beautiful lady and a man walking hand in hand towards him.

"Hello," he called to them smiling in innocence, "Who are you?"

"Anna and Raven, but you must go back my child, go back," said the shining lady.

"Can't I stay and play with you? You are so shiny and light," said Noah.

"No. There are many years must pass before you can come where we are. Go home to your parents," said Raven.

Then Anna and Raven turned away and walked out into the moor until they disappeared.

Noah ran back to the farm to tell his mother.

"Mummy, mummy, I met a beautiful lady and a man on the moor. They were called Anna and Raven."

"No Noah, no. I have heard they used to live here a long time ago. They are long dead Noah. You must have been imagining things. Maybe you heard Daddy and I talking about them. But you mustn't go on to the moor alone. Stay in the garden. It can be dangerous."

She scooped him up, kissed him and hugged him tight.

Life went on at Dragon Fell Farm. The moor was still there. Odinsdale endured as it always had, cold, bleak and starkly beautiful. The dragon had a new child to protect now. He breathed on Noah and kept him safe through the cold winters. All was well. In the village, some mothers still tell their children not to walk on the moor alone or the beautiful lady and her lover may take them away into the other world.

"Behave yourselves, or evil Raven will come for you," is the cry of many an exasperated mother.

Anna's grave lies still at the edge of the grounds of Odinsdale Hall. It is now covered in moss and lichen. A family of rabbits has made their home nearby in a warren with many holes in evidence with little creatures poking their noses into the air. Crows and ravens call to each other from the yew trees and bats play around the grave on moonlit nights. The owls hoot their secrets to each other.

The moor is busy encroaching on to the Hall land. The heather has managed to push down part of the stone wall and plant itself all around the graveyard. Brambles are wrapping themselves around the headstone and nettles obscure the writing on it.

"All is well, and all manner of things shall be well." from Revelations of Divine Love by Julian of Norwich is the inscription on the gravestone that is still able to be read to this day.